Easter Buried Eggs

A Black Cat Café Cozy Mystery Series

by Lyndsey Cole

Connect with me:

Lyndsey@LyndseyColeBooks.com

www.facebook.com/LyndseyColeAuthor

CHAPTER 1

Annie ran to the Black Cat Café door with the smell of burnt sweetness filling her nose and panic surging through her body. One look at Leona's face told Annie that her aunt was right on the edge of a meltdown, following close behind the smoky mess she held in her hand.

A pan flew across the kitchen, barely missing a window before it crashed against the wall. A string of words that no one should hear first thing in the morning followed the ear-tingling clang. Annie considered turning around before she was sucked into whatever disaster was cooking in Leona's world.

"The Golden Living retirement home will be the death of me," Leona said after a wooden spoon landed on top of the growing mess on the floor.

Annie poured two coffees and sat at the counter. "Time out, Leona. Take a deep breath and sit down for five minutes." She glanced out the French doors to the view of Heron Lake with New Hampshire's White Mountains beyond. The lake sparkled with reflecting sunshine.

"A break is *exactly* what I need." She threw her apron on the floor which, at least, landed silently.

Annie couldn't help but wonder what Leona's words meant—a five-minute break like Annie suggested, or a longer break which would create many problems at the Black Cat Café.

"And I plan to take it," Leona added without making anything clear at all. "I've been working seven long days a week and I'm fed up. You've been helping me here, Annie, and it's time you step it up and run the place while Danny and I take a few days off."

Annie swallowed, but a lump somewhere on the way down choked her. Her eyes watered as panic set in. How could she say no? Leona was right about needing some time off, after all, but Annie wasn't sure if she could handle all the responsibility. Sure, she was comfortable working *with* Leona, but being in charge was a completely different pile of eggs.

And she didn't think she could handle all that delicate juggling.

"Maybe you should wait until after the Golden Living Easter dinner. You know, when it slows down a little," Annie tentatively suggested, hoping to feel out Leona's level of desperation.

A glare met her words. Okay, Leona's need for some time off must be a nine-and-a-half out of ten.

"You're not up to it, Annie?" Leona demanded to know.

"Of course I am." She silently added a *not* at the end of the sentence as she smiled at her aunt. She mentally went down the to-do list for the rest of the day—dye eggs for the Easter baskets, prepare and organize the food for the Easter dinner, and cater the dinner for the seniors at the Golden Living retirement home. Plus, all the normal baking and daily café operations to take care of. No, of course she wasn't at all sure if she could handle it alone. "You and Danny take a day off, I'll be fine." The words came out of her mouth unbidden.

Leona's glare turned into a glower. "We're leaving until Friday. Deal with it." She picked up her apron and handed it to Annie. "And, by the way, I burned the cake for the dinner tonight, so you'll have to start from scratch to get the Easter bunny cake done, frosted, and ready to go with the ham, pineapple, scalloped potatoes, and green beans."

Leona sighed and sat next to Annie. She picked up her cup of coffee. "Good idea. I feel better already." She sipped the hot coffee. "Now I'm ready to take a five-minute break with you before you get to work."

Annie stared at Leona. This couldn't be happening. How did she let herself get steamrolled into this burden when a simple 'no' would have saved her?

"Sorry for the outburst. I guess something snapped when I smelled that burnt cake and you were the one to walk in...wrong place at the wrong time." The new and improved Leona smiled. "Don't look so worried. You'll be fine." She gave Annie a quick hug. "And thank you."

Annie sipped her coffee, the only activity she could manage after the shock she just received. "I wish I had the confidence in me that you have. To be honest, I'm not sure I feel up to the responsibility. What if I completely muck it all up?"

Leona swiveled her seat to face Annie. "You think no one ever makes a mistake?"

"Of course not." But she added to herself that *she* didn't make mistakes. "I don't want to disappoint you."

"I think the only one you will disappoint is yourself. Put on the apron, turn on the radio, and pretend you're me if that helps you get through the day." Leona laughed. "Boy, I feel like a weight fell off my shoulders. I sure am looking forward to leaving so I can get back."

Leona turned on the radio to her favorite oldies station. "There, one less thing for you to do." And with her parting optimism, Leona said, "What could go wrong?"

Annie mumbled several thoughts in that department as she fastened a green apron decorated with black cats, curled up napping. "*I* could burn the cake or *I* could trip and break my leg, or *I* could crash on my way to Golden Living with the whole dinner getting destroyed and all the seniors waiting for hours for food."

"Or everything will go smooth as chocolate pudding," Annie's mother said as she more or less snuck up behind Annie. "Leona told me the change in plans on her way out. Where did all this doubt come from?"

Annie shrugged.

"Well?"

"Apparently, I hide it well."

Mia snorted. "It's high time you get yourself out of that comfort zone of letting Leona make all the decisions around here and see that you are more than capable of handling anything that comes along."

Annie frowned.

"It's not the end of the world if everything isn't absolutely perfect. You just move on and make the most of it." Mia tied a red apron with jumping black cats around her waist. "What are we starting with?"

"The cake." A small grin bloomed into a big smile before a giggle escaped. "Did Leona tell you about her disaster?"

"Nope."

Annie pointed to the floor next to the window. "She burned her cake and had a meltdown."

"Ahhh. So you're afraid that's where you'll be heading if something goes wrong?"

"I guess so."

"Let me tell you something about my sister: She could never handle any type of disaster and I had to clean up her messes."

"Too bad you didn't walk in before I did," Annie said as she took the broom out of the closet. "That would have saved me a lot of stress."

Mia fixed herself a cup of coffee while Annie cleaned up the smashed cake. "Leona wouldn't have asked me to take over so she could leave. She knows you can handle the responsibility. You just need a little push. Don't worry, I'll help."

"Everyone keeps saying, 'don't worry,' but I do worry. I worry that I'll forget something important. I worry that I'll screw up her business. What then?"

Mia waved her hand dismissively. "Just do your best. That's all anyone can expect."

Annie dumped the ruined cake in the trash, got a mop, and washed the floor. Mia got out the ingredients for the cake but left it for Annie while she turned off the radio and attended to the first arrivals for their Wednesday morning.

It was normally Annie's responsibility to handle the pastry display and the drink cart, but Mia took all that over so Annie could work on the cake and food for the seniors' Easter dinner. She actually enjoyed the concentration and lack of interruptions.

While the carrot cake baked, she sliced what felt like a ton of potatoes for two huge trays of scalloped potatoes. "If these disappear I'll be surprised, but this is how many Leona said to make."

"The staff can dig in, too. It's always a good idea to think about the help. They appreciate it and you never know when they might be able to do a favor back," Mia told Annie.

Annie felt some of her earlier trepidation disappear as the morning flew by. Maybe she'd overreacted when Leona dumped all this in her lap. Maybe she was better at managing than she realized.

The phone rang.

"The Black Cat Café," Annie answered in her most professional, cheerful voice.

"Ms. Cross here."

"What can I do for you, Ms. Cross?" Annie held the phone between her shoulder and her ear while she covered one tray of scalloped potatoes with foil.

"You were supposed to call me to find out how many seniors signed up for the dinner."

Apparently, Leona forgot to mention this little detail. Her brain buzzed while she tried to figure out how to deal with this angry woman.

"Is this Leona? I need to talk to Leona."

"No, Leona can't come to the phone." Annie's heart fluttered with anxiety. "This is Annie Hunter." Ms. Cross, who Leona usually only referred to as Dawn, was impatiently waiting on the other end of the phone. The stern image of the manager of Golden Living popped into Annie's head. "How can I help you?"

"Are you sure you're capable of helping me? It doesn't sound like you have a clue about the dinner Leona promised to cater tonight."

With the phone securely anchored between her shoulder and ear, Annie wiped her sweaty hands on her apron.

A long sigh blasted in Annie's ear and Dawn continued. "I guess you'll have to do. There's been a change. We need a vegetarian entrée for two added in. The total number for the dinner will be thirty-five. The bunny starts in the photo booth at three-thirty while you serve the hors d'oeuvres and drinks. Dinner at four-thirty. I want it all wrapped up by six. Understand?" A sound like someone tapping long fingernails against the phone met Annie's ear.

Annie scribbled all the last-minute instructions in Leona's daily diary, hoping she didn't miss anything but refusing to ask Dawn to repeat herself.

"Well?"

"Yes. No problem."

"Oh, and add chocolate and vanilla ice cream for the cake. Everyone has requested ice cream. With those little chocolate sprinkles. They probably won't even eat the cake; hope you didn't go to too much trouble on that."

Right, the cake that *started* all the trouble. Annie began to say okay but realized the call was disconnected. She looked at the phone. Great. This was exactly what she was worried about. The dinner at the Golden Living retirement home was going to be a disaster.

CHAPTER 2

By the time Annie parked the Black Cat Café van at the Golden Living loading dock, she was already exhausted. How did Leona do it day after day? She had never realized how draining all the work *plus* thinking about every single detail actually was. She did feel an itsy-bitsy spark of pride, though, in managing to get all the food prepared without mishap and packed in the van without spilling a drip of anything.

"Need help?" a voice asked.

Annie turned and stared into a huge fake smile, forever set in a white face with two long white fuzzy ears with pink in the middle, bobbing over the entire fuzzy white outfit.

"The Easter bunny?"

"No kidding, were you expecting Santa, maybe?" The Easter bunny stuck his fuzzy paw toward Annie. "Forrest. And please, no jokes about my name, I've heard them all. Dawn told me to help you."

Annie shook Forrest's hand. "Maybe you could show me where I'm supposed to set everything up. I can manage once I know where I'm working, and I'd hate to have anything spill on your bunny fur."

Forrest quickly looked down and brushed an imaginary piece of something off his fake fur. "Don't worry about it. Glad to have something to do before the seniors start pawing all over me." He tipped his bunny face back to reveal a grin. "Get it? Paw all over me?"

Annie rolled her eyes. "You probably make their day. A cute bunny making silly jokes. What more could they ask for?"

"Delicious food? I think that's really the highlight of their existence." He moved toward the door. "Come on. I'll show you where the kitchen is and help you move all your stuff. Don't you have anyone helping you?"

Annie glanced down the driveway. "A couple people should be here any minute." As she followed Forrest, she did wonder where her mother and Martha were. Mia was picking up the jelly beans for the last-minute cake decorations that Leona seemed to have forgotten or misplaced—or took with her on her impromptu vacation—and two flower arrangements from The Enchanted Florist. Martha, her sixtyish, always-ready-for-anything friend, had volunteered to help since her childhood best friend, Sylvia, lived at the Golden Living retirement home. Apparently, the two of them managed to cause some drama whenever they were together. Annie silently made a wish that they would be on their best behavior tonight.

Forrest held the door open to a gleaming, stainless steel kitchen with all the bells and whistles that any cook would love to have. Annie whistled her approval. "And which door leads to the dining area?"

Forrest laid his bunny head, paws, and floppy feet on a counter. "Right through here." He pushed open a swinging door to a lovely room with round tables, each covered with a white tablecloth, a potted hyacinth, silverware, and water goblets for four people. Around one side of the room, long folding tables were available for Annie to set up her warming trays for the dinner.

"And over here," Forrest gestured, "is the photo booth. You brought Easter eggs, didn't you? That will make a nice prop for people to hold while they have their picture taken with me."

Annie nodded. "Colored eggs, chocolate eggs, and plastic eggs with surprises inside. Plus, little baskets to set at each place filled with grass, one chocolate Easter bunny, and a couple of those marshmallow peeps."

"Sounds like sugar overload but, when you're retired, I guess you should be able to eat whatever you want."

The door from the kitchen opened. "Here you are," Martha said. "I never came in through the back door before." She looked around the room. "Nice set up, don't you think? Sylvia is very excited for this dinner."

"Great, let's get the van unpacked." Annie walked toward the kitchen.

"Forrest? You're the Easter bunny?" Martha asked. "You did such a great job as Cupid for Valentine's Day, I'm not surprised to see you here again."

"I'm pretty sure I wasn't Her Highness's first choice, but," he shrugged, "I take what I can get."

Martha put one hand around her mouth and whispered, "You must be referring to Dawn?"

Forrest nodded. "She's a tough one and she may have only hired me for this gig because a bunch of the seniors requested me. That's fine. I'll get my check before I leave and be done with her."

Annie opened the van's side door and directed what everyone could carry inside. When she unloaded the cake, Mia pulled up next to the van. "Posie McBride outdid herself for this event. She's probably hoping for some repeat business for The Enchanted Florist from these folks and their families."

"A bit underhanded of a motive to give Leona such a good price, but she has to look ahead for future business," Annie said. "Follow me."

Mia carried one basket filled with spring flowers— tulips, lilies, pussy willows, and lime green hydrangeas—set it on the buffet, and returned for the other one.

When she returned, she whispered to Annie, "Still full of self-doubt? It looks to me like everything is coming together nicely."

"I've already gained a big appreciation for all that Leona juggles, but to answer your question, my confidence bounces around more than a yo-yo. So far, I feel like I'm in control, but in five minutes? Everything could be chaos."

Mia laughed. "This is the perfect event for you to get a taste of running the show. I know Leona has been wanting to take some time off and, really, when is it ever the *right* time? You have to jump in and figure it out." She gave her daughter a quick hug of encouragement. "You'll do just fine."

With those words ringing in her ears, Annie let her concentration down for two seconds. An ear-splitting crash from behind the kitchen door echoed into the dining room. She dashed into the kitchen to find one pan of scalloped potatoes oozing over the shiny white tiles and two bunny feet. Her heart plummeted into her stomach.

Forrest had eyes as big as the white fluffy tail on the back of his costume when he looked at Annie. "Oops. I was getting my head back on and I must have knocked into that tray." He lowered his voice. "How about I scoop it back into the pan?"

As appealing as that suggestion was, Annie had the sense to know it was a terrible idea. "Just get out." She pointed to the door. "I'll clean up and figure something out." What the solution would be, she had no idea. Maybe this crowd wouldn't like the scalloped potatoes, anyway, and the one remaining tray would be enough.

Mia rushed through the door. Her mouth flopped open like a fish gasping for air when she saw the mess. "What?" She composed herself and tried to smooth over the food problem. "Not the end of the world. We do the serving, so I'll be sure to use a small spoon and make the one pan of scalloped potatoes stretch to everyone who wants some."

Annie checked the time. She had an hour and a half to finish the cake, get the food on the buffet tables, and at the same time, serve the hors d'oeuvres. She took a deep, calming breath while Mia and Martha stared at her, waiting for instructions. "Martha, you can offer drinks to everyone when they arrive and while they're milling around talking or waiting for a turn in the photo booth. Mom, you can serve the hors d'oeuvres. I need about ten minutes to finish putting the face on the cake. At four-fifteen, we'll carry all the food out to the warming trays so we can start serving at four-thirty."

Mia and Martha nodded.

Martha reached into her big tote that she had stored out of the way. "I made these aprons for us to wear, you know, so we don't just blend in with the residents.

I guess Mia and I might be the only ones that need to worry about that." She handed out bright green aprons with bunnies hopping among red and yellow tulips. "What do you think?"

"Personally, I prefer the aprons you made for the café covered with black cats in every pose imaginable, but these are perfect for this event," Annie said as she tied one around her waist. "Have the Easter baskets been placed next to everyone's place?"

"I didn't see any," Mia said. "Are you sure you brought them?"

"I'll check the van and bring them out." She ran her fingers through her strawberry blond curls. "Everything will be fine," she added, more for herself than the other two women who were already headed to the dining room.

The Easter baskets were in the van, piled on the passenger seat and on the floor in front of the seat. No wonder no one remembered them. It only took a few minutes for Annie to distribute them around the tables. It also gave her a chance to see the guests. At least they all seemed to be in a festive mood. For now.

Uh-oh, she saw trouble heading her way. Annie steeled her shoulders and put on a friendly smile. "Hello Ms. Cross." What a fitting name, Annie said to herself.

"Dawn, please." She lightly touched Annie's arm. "Everything looks quite nice. I wasn't sure you'd be able to pull it off after I talked to you on the phone earlier. I'll be mingling with the seniors if you need me for anything."

Maybe she wasn't so bad, Annie thought as she returned to the kitchen.

Annie popped a black jelly bean in her mouth and studied her cake after she finished applying the jelly bean face. She had to admit that she was proud of how the bunny came out. With coconut sticking all willy-nilly in the cream cheese frosting and the black jelly bean eyes, nose, and pink mouth, it looked too good to eat. She even had the bunny resting on a nest of dyed-green coconut. All in all, it was as good as Leona would have produced. Or maybe even better, she told herself proudly.

Annie carefully carried the ham to the buffet table, followed by the pan of scalloped potatoes and the green beans. Mustard, rolls, and butter were placed at the end for the diners to take as needed. After she put the cake in the most visible spot, she checked the time and had a good fifteen minutes to mingle before serving the food.

Annie turned around and bumped into Martha.

"I want you to meet my best friend forever, Sylvia. We've known each other ever since her family moved in next door to mine."

"You led me into all kinds of trouble, Martha. And since you're younger, *I* was the one who always got the blame."

"Hehehe," Martha giggled. "What are we going to do tonight to liven up these old people? Switch the name tags? Photo bomb the Easter pictures? How about some rock and roll songs instead of these old love ballads?"

Annie held Martha's arm. "Don't mess it up for me. Leona trusted me to manage this dinner and I need everything to go as smooth as silky bunny fur."

Sylvia elbowed her friend. "Here comes Marvin. He could be your partner in crime. He's always sneaking around this place snooping on everyone. As far as I know, he hasn't made too many friends, especially not with Dawn or the secretary, Gloria."

"Marvin." Sylvia waved to get his attention. "Come meet my friends."

Marvin glanced around the room before he walked any closer. He maneuvered along the edge of the people, keeping his back to the wall.

"A bit paranoid?" Annie asked.

Sylvia leaned close to Annie. "Dawn has written him up for sneaking around at night after we're all supposed to be asleep, or at least in our apartments."

"What's he looking for?"

Sylvia shrugged. "He told me he just likes to keep an eye on everything."

Marvin silently edged his way next to Sylvia. "I don't like the kid in the bunny costume. Why is he here again? Last time he stole my money."

"That was never proven, Marvin. Didn't your son think maybe you misplaced it?" Sylvia gently reminded Marvin.

"Forrest told me that he was surprised that Dawn hired him. I got the feeling there is bad blood between those two," Annie said, wondering what, if anything, happened between Forrest and Dawn.

Marvin leaned close to Annie. "Who are you?"

"Oh," Martha said. "Marvin, this is my friend, Annie. She's in charge of the dinner tonight. Try to be nice to her, okay?"

"Did you put poison in anything?" He kept his steely gray eyes on Annie's face.

She leaned her head as far away from Marvin as possible. "Of course not."

"No, I suppose you have no reason to poison any of us, but that Easter bunny, I'm not so sure about him. Was he near the food?"

Sylvia rolled her eyes. "Oh Marvin. Forrest just hasn't figured out what he wants to do with his life yet. He's harmless."

"You like everyone, Sylvia. I've seen things around this place and you're going to find yourself in trouble if you aren't more careful." Marvin walked away from the women, found his name tag, and switched it with one from another table.

"He's really not so bad once you get used to him," Sylvia said. "He kind of grows on you over time."

"Lock your door at night," Martha told her friend. "With people like that wandering around, you can't be too careful.

CHAPTER 3

At one minute before four-thirty, Dawn rang a little bell. "The food is hot. Get in line or go hungry."

Annie had the two vegetarian meals—half of a zucchini stuffed with rice and peppers, with tomato and cheese melted on top—tucked off to one side, not sure who they were for, but she assumed someone would ask for them.

Marvin was first in line. "I don't want the leftovers. Or any food that someone has touched."

Annie served him a piece of ham topped with a fresh pineapple slice, Mia dished out some scalloped potatoes, and Martha added a scoop of green beans to his plate. He used the tongs to grab a roll before he sat down, meticulously spread his napkin on his lap, and took a sip from his water goblet.

A man with some obsessive-compulsive tendencies, Annie observed before her attention returned to the line of hungry people.

With guests holding plates out as fast as Annie could serve, the ham began to disappear but she knew there was no way she would run out. Unfortunately, she was not as confident about the scalloped potatoes, but her mother gave her a thumbs-up when she glanced over. Nothing she could do about it at this point if they didn't have enough.

Silverware clinked against the china and a noisy murmur of multiple conversations rose above the quiet background music, giving an impression that all was under control.

"Did you bring a vegetarian choice?"

Annie looked up to see a short woman staring through her bifocals. "I was thinking Dawn made a mistake since no one asked yet. Here you go." Annie slid the stuffed zucchini onto the offered plate.

"I wasn't sure she would remember. She's not too happy with me at the moment. Nice spread, by the way."

"You live here?" Annie asked.

The woman laughed. "Sometimes it feels like I do with the hours I put in, but no, I'm the lowly secretary."

Annie lowered her voice and checked to be sure Dawn was not within hearing distance. "You probably run the place."

"I like you. My name's Gloria, by the way. I saw you were talking to Sylvia earlier—she's a sweetheart. And Marvin—" Gloria's eyes rolled up so high, Annie wasn't sure they'd come back. "A creeper."

"A creeper?"

"Yeah, he turns up when you least expect him. He walks around with some kind of special shoes that don't make a sound. It gives me the creeps." She shuddered. "But what can I do? He lives here, pays his bills, or at least his son pays his bills, so I have to put up with his weirdness." She looked at her plate. "So, what is this you made?"

"Stuffed zucchini. I hope you like it."

"Yum. I'm drooling already. This, some scalloped potatoes, green beans, and a slice of that cake will make me feel like I'm in heaven."

"Wait a minute before you sit down," Annie said. "Dawn asked me to make two vegetarian entrees, do you know who the other one is for?"

"Oh, that must be for Sean. He doesn't eat in the dining room. If you wrap it up, I'll leave it in on my desk for him to pick up."

"Sure. No problem. I have a reusable container I can put it in with everything else and all he'll have to do is pop it in the microwave after he takes out the cake." Annie loaded up the container, stretched the yellow silicone cover on, and handed Gloria the meal. She watched as Gloria juggled her plate and the extra entree while she wobbled precariously on her high heels toward a table off to one side. She made it without mishap.

Annie looked over the dining tables at everyone talking, eating, or just sitting quietly. Marvin was at a table with Sylvia and two other women. While Annie watched, Marvin stabbed his fork into his roll, cut it in half, and wiped his plate, never touching his food with his fingers. A creeper and a germaphobe?

Forrest stuck a plate in front of Annie. His bunny head and paws were missing. "Anything left for a hungry Easter bunny?"

"Sure, let me grab my bag of carrots." She reached under the table.

"Ah, seriously?"

Annie laughed. "Just kidding." She slid two big slices of ham onto his plate. "No scalloped potatoes for you, though."

"Really?"

Mia held out a small scoop. "Just enough for one last serving."

Forrest smiled. "I'm glad *someone* has some compassion around here."

"What's that supposed to mean?" Annie asked.

Forrest gave an almost imperceptible head nod toward the table where Dawn seemed to be keeping her eyes over the diners. "I won't name anyone, but someone can't wait for me to get out of here. Little does she know, I'm not leaving without a paycheck." He leaned close to Annie. "Have you been paid already?"

"Half when she reserved the date and half after we clean up. Should I be worried?"

"Let me put it this way, don't let her give you any excuse that she can't pay tonight. I know she has a safe full of cash that she hates to part with."

"Thanks for the tip. Don't forget to come back for dessert."

Forrest glanced at the cake with a piece missing for Sean. "Looks too nice to eat. Besides, I'm not sure I'd feel right about chomping into one of my relatives." He tried to suppress his lips from twitching up into a grin but failed miserably. "I'll be in the photo booth eating. Stop by if you fancy a photo with your favorite Easter bunny." He winked at Annie and walked around the tables and disappeared in his booth.

Martha and Mia brought the warming trays into the kitchen before they stacked plates and cleared tables to make room for dessert. Annie brought out the ice cream to soften for easier scooping.

Unsurprisingly, Marvin was the first in line. "I want the tip of the ear with a scoop of vanilla ice cream on the left, chocolate on the right, and those sprinkles on everything."

After Annie filled his request, he poked at the cake with his fork. "What's all the bumpy stuff?"

"Coconut."

"Are you sure?"

"Yes. I think I should know what I used when I made the cake, Marvin." Annie tried to keep her growing annoyance out of her tone.

He stuck a piece on his tongue. "Tastes sweet. I guess I'll eat it." He returned to his seat, taking a bit of vanilla ice cream, cake, then chocolate ice cream on his fork with each bite.

To each his own, Annie decided. She wouldn't have to deal with the likes of Marvin after tonight.

The cake shrank on its platter and the ice cream disappeared by the time the last diner held out a plate.

"No leftovers of that cake?" Dawn appeared after everyone else had been served. "There's usually leftovers."

"One ear is left and all the coconut nest, plus lots of jelly beans," Annie said.

"Wrap it up for me so I can take it home. I want to get out of here as soon as possible."

Annie stopped with the bunny ear half-way between the platter and a smaller plate. "I need you to write a check for the balance due before you leave."

"Not until everything is cleaned. That was the agreement. Stop at my office when you're done. I'm heading there now." Dawn took the plate and left the room.

"What do I do now?" Annie asked her mother. "What if she doesn't wait around to pay me?" Annie sizzled inside. This being-in-charge certainly presented more problems than jelly beans in an Easter basket.

"Let's get busy so Dawn leaving before you are paid doesn't become an issue." Mia carried the empty ice cream containers to the kitchen.

Marvin and Sylvia were long gone and the last of the slowest stragglers were on their way out of the dining room followed by Forrest. On his way to Dawn's office, Annie guessed. At least he had a good chance of getting paid, Annie said to herself. She stacked the dessert plates and carried them into the kitchen. Mia had the clean dinner dishes unloaded from the dishwasher and ready for the last load of dirty dishes.

"Sylvia said your dinner was one of the best they've had here," Martha said as she dried one of Annie's big warming trays. "Everyone loved the cake."

"Good to hear, especially after half the scalloped potatoes ended up on the floor. I hope everyone got enough."

"No complaints. Well, except for Marvin, but Sylvia said to ignore him. He rarely says anything good about anything."

"What did he complain about?" Annie asked.

"Just a couple of things—the ham was too salty, the potatoes were overcooked, and the cake was too sweet. But he loved the ice cream. Or maybe he complained that it was too cold." Martha laughed. "I think that covers all his comments."

"Ha. The one thing I didn't make is all that might have gotten a compliment. He's a strange one. You said Sylvia and Marvin are friends?"

Martha stacked the clean trays. "Yes, they are friends because Sylvia manages to find something positive about everyone. One of her faults, as far as I'm concerned. She tends to overlook some glaring bad qualities in people."

"What does she overlook with Marvin?"

"He seems to have a conspiracy theory about everything, starting with Forrest stealing from his room during the last event here. He can't let anything go, but Sylvia doesn't mind," Martha explained.

Annie leaned against the gleaming stainless counter. "With the short time I was here, I got the distinct impression that Gloria isn't a fan of Marvin. She actually used the word 'creeper' when she mentioned him."

"I promised myself I wouldn't start any gossiping while we were here working, but," Martha peeked out the door into the dining room, "since you've started it, I'll fill you in on what Sylvia told me. Gloria has her own issues to worry about."

Annie raised her eyebrows and waited for Martha to continue.

"Everyone thinks she's addicted to prescription pain pills."

"Who's everyone?"

"Well, Sylvia heard it from Forrest under strict confidentiality. He likes to have something on everyone, in case he needs to put a little pressure on to get what he wants."

"Forrest sounds like a manipulative, scheming guy. I thought he was harmless, but now I'm not so sure. What else do you know?" Annie asked.

Martha's phone beeped at six-fifty with a text message. "It's from Sylvia. She's probably wondering where I am. I told her I'd meet her in her apartment when we finished up here." Martha tapped her screen. Her mouth fell open.

Annie peered over her shoulder. "What is it? Your face is as white as the Easter bunny's fur."

Martha handed her phone to Annie. She read the message, *Come to Dawn's office...sounded like a gunshot.*

Annie rushed through the door into the dining area. She stopped so suddenly, Martha smacked right into her back. Annie turned around and caught Martha before she crumpled on the floor.

"Where's Dawn's office? You have to lead the way, Martha."

Martha grabbed Annie's arm and pulled her down the hall to the end, then turned left. The front entryway was well-lit in front of them with a big glass window and a door to the right.

Martha pointed. "That's Dawn's office. It's dark. What should we do?"

Mia caught up to Martha and Annie. "What's going on?"

"Shhh!"

They huddled against the wall. Martha told Mia what Sylvia texted. Annie put her hand on the office door.

Mia pulled her back. "What are you doing? What if someone is still in there with a gun?"

Martha handed her phone to Annie. "Send Sylvia another message."

Where are you? Annie typed.

In the supply closet, came back immediately.

In Dawn's office? We are in the hall. Is it safe to come in?

I don't know. I heard a door slam and now it's quiet. Help me. I'm scared. In Dawn's office.

Annie gave the phone back to Martha. "Call Deputy Christy Crank and tell her there's been a gunshot here. I'm going inside to find Sylvia."

She turned the doorknob.

She pulled the door open, inch by inch.

A heavy silence filled the dark office.

CHAPTER 4

"There's a light switch on the right, just inside the door," Martha whispered to Annie.

Annie's arm slinked around the door frame into the office and her fingers slid up and down, feeling for a switch.

With one small movement, a bright white glow filled the room and sliced a path out into the hallway.

All was silent except for the slight buzzing of the overhead bulbs.

A whiff of potatoes drifted to her nose.

She eased her head far enough to her left so her eyes could peer inside. A big desk faced her. A gaping wide open safe drew her attention. What had Forrest said to her? Something about Dawn keeping a lot of cash in her safe. Well, the safe she was looking at held a stack of folders but she couldn't see any cash.

Her eyes moved from the safe to the floor.

She flung her head back to the safety of the hall and covered her mouth. Both Mia and Martha stared at her with wide questioning eyes.

Annie let herself take another look. One bunny foot, smeared with dried scalloped potatoes, poked out from behind the desk. Was that foot connected to anything?

The rest of the office looked to be in order. She heard a small sob come from behind a door.

"Sylvia?" Annie, forgetting her fear, rushed to the door and yanked it open.

Martha's friend was crouching in the corner, under a shelf crowded with reams of paper. She let out a sigh when her eyes met Annie's. "What happened?"

Annie held out her hand to help Sylvia stand. She had to hobble forward before she had room to straighten.

"Are you okay?" Annie asked.

Sylvia nodded. "I heard someone coming in so I hid in here."

"But why?"

Sylvia's face burned red with embarrassment. "I needed to talk to Dawn about my, um, financial situation."

Before Sylvia could finish her explanation, Martha interrupted. "Annie, come take a look over here."

The image of the bunny foot returned to her brain as she moved closer to where Martha stood, staring at something behind the desk.

The four women gawked.

Martha broke the silence. "Looks like the Easter bunny met a hunter."

A squeak escaped from Sylvia before she slumped to the floor.

Footsteps sounded in the hall and all of the women's heads turned in unison.

"Having a little tea party, ladies?" Detective Christy Crank asked as she entered the room.

Annie moved to one side to make room for the detective. "No, that's not exactly how I would describe the problem here."

"The Easter bunny? Anyone know who's inside the costume?"

"Forrest. He was at the Easter dinner tonight, for photos with the guests," Annie explained.

"And the rest of you? Delivering Easter eggs or something like that?"

"Sort of." Annie knew she shouldn't give a smart answer, but sometimes Christy Crank brought the worst out in her. And after the way her day was ending, it wouldn't take much to let her tongue get the better of her.

Christy was on her phone, ignoring Annie for the moment, as she called for more police, emergency, and crime scene personnel. The Golden Living retirement home would be crawling with people searching every inch of the premises and Annie had a sinking feeling that she wouldn't be heading back to the comfort of her bed for much longer than she would like.

"Okay," Christy said as she turned back toward Annie. "Fill me in."

"I don't know what happened. Sylvia," Annie pointed to Martha's friend who was beginning to recover on one of the office chairs. "She heard what she thought was a gunshot so we came to help her." Annie decided to let Sylvia give Christy the details of why she was in the closet in the first place. There was no doubt in Annie's mind that it would leave Sylvia in a position reeking with guilt.

"Listen, Annie, you have a habit of ending up nearby whenever there's a body in Catfish Cove, so either tell me everything you know now or you'll be sitting on that hard chair until your butt screams for a pillow." Christy crossed her arms, jiggled her right leg up and down, cocked her head, and waited for two seconds. "Well?"

"All I know is that Forrest," she pointed to the body, "told me he needed to go to Dawn's office to get paid for his Easter bunny job tonight."

Christy scribbled in her notebook. "Dawn?"

"Dawn Cross, the manager of this place."

"Where's Dawn?"

Annie shrugged. "No one else was in here when I turned the light on. I wrapped up the leftover Easter cake for her when dinner was over in the dining room and she said she was going to her office, then heading home to eat the cake."

"Why are you three," Christy included Mia and Martha, "still here if the dinner is over?"

"Cleaning up."

Christy scribbled more notes. She tapped her pen against her jaw. "Is this the sequence of events? An Easter dinner, the Easter bunny went to the office to get paid, someone heard a gunshot, you came, and the Easter bunny was already dead on the floor."

"In a nutshell, that's all I know."

"What's her story?" Christy pointed to Sylvia.

"Sylvia lives here. She's the one who heard the gunshot."

Before Christy could interrogate Sylvia, the crime scene crew arrived. Christy ushered Annie, Mia, Martha, and Sylvia into the hallway, and with a smile on her face, she told them to sit tight.

"Ma'am? Can we wait in my apartment?" Sylvia asked in a meek voice.

Oh great. Annie knew that one label Christy Crank hated more than being called 'Cranky' was when someone called her 'Ma'am.'

"Excuse me?" Christy slowly pivoted on one foot and glared at Sylvia. Annie couldn't help but feel extreme sympathy for the elderly woman at that moment.

"My apartment is down that hallway." Sylvia pointed. "Can we wait there? With the door open?"

Annie gave Sylvia credit for being able to face down Christy's glare without cracking like an Easter egg rolling off the counter.

"Show me."

Sylvia led the way to her door, opened it, and waited for Christy to make her decision. "Okay. But don't set one foot out of here. Understand?"

Everyone nodded.

Sylvia entered, turned a lamp on, and offered seats to the others. "It isn't much. I only have this small sitting-dining area and my tiny kitchen, my bedroom, and bathroom, but it will be better than sitting on that cold, hard floor." She stood, wringing her hands, waiting for the other women to respond.

Martha was the first to find her voice. "I don't know about the rest of you, but I need to pee. I didn't dare ask Christy for a bathroom break."

Annie and Mia sat side by side on Sylvia's dark red loveseat, which left a recliner and a wooden rocking chair for Sylvia and Martha.

Sylvia sat in the rocking chair. "I'm sorry I got you in this mess. I was so scared, I didn't know what else to do." She rocked back and forth.

Annie leaned forward. "About that. Why were you in the closet to begin with?"

"Oh dear. I don't know where to begin." She rocked faster.

Martha returned and plopped into the recliner. "Spill it Sylvia. I can't believe you got yourself into that mess without me by your side."

"Oh, Martha. You know how I told you I might be moving?"

"Yes, but you never told me why. I thought you loved your little apartment here and having all the other folks around to hang out with."

Sylvia nodded. "I do love it here. That's the problem. I've got some money problems and I went to talk to Dawn to see if there was any kind of subsidy available or if she could give me extra time to pay my monthly fees."

"I bet that went over like a rotten Easter egg. From what you've told me about Dawn, she squeezes every nickel to death. Twice."

"When I first talked to her, it didn't go well, so I went back but I never actually saw her. When I went into the office, the safe was open. All I could see was a stack of folders. When I was in there this morning, she hadn't closed it properly and I saw a lot of cash inside. Do you think someone robbed her safe?"

"And killed Forrest?" Annie asked.

"Forrest wasn't in there yet. No one was in the office, but I heard footsteps slapping down the hallway toward the office and I panicked. That's when I hid in the closet."

The four women jumped when a bang, bang, bang sounded on Sylvia's open door.

Sylvia's hand flew to her chest, then dropped back into her lap. "It's only Marvin," she said to the others. "Detective Crank didn't say I couldn't have a visitor, did she?"

Martha patted Sylvia's hand. "Don't be such a worrywart. Come on in, Marvin."

Annie rubbed her forehead. Would she be in this mess if Leona hadn't decided to take a few days off? Would she be in this mess if she had just left instead of worrying about getting paid?

But she did feel some sympathy for Sylvia, who was the one in the biggest mess of all of them.

Sylvia fidgeted in her rocking chair, clasping and unclasping her hands. Her eyes darted around her small apartment. Did she understand how Detective Christy Crank would put the pieces together at the crime scene, with Sylvia front and center? Sylvia was in the closet when Forrest was murdered, she knew about the money in the safe, and she was about to be kicked out of her apartment.

Oh boy. Sylvia needed a lot of help, but she didn't even know it yet.

Marvin looked at each face staring at him before he settled his eyes on Sylvia. "I saw you go into the office minutes before Forrest entered. Now he's dead." And just as silently as he'd arrived, Marvin disappeared.

"Sylvia?" Annie looked at the tiny woman. "Do you own a gun?"

"Oh dear. I should have reported that it was stolen last week, but I never did tell anyone. Do you think that's a problem?"

It wasn't so much a problem, but more like the icing on the hot cross buns as far as Detective Crank would be concerned.

"Don't worry," Annie said, hating those two words even more than when they had been directed at her that morning.

CHAPTER 5

Detective Christy Crank walked into Sylvia's apartment liked she owned the place. She picked up a magazine on the small table next to the recliner. "A travel guide. Someone has a trip planned?" She raised her eyes and stared at Sylvia.

A pink blush crept into Sylvia's cheeks. "I like to dream about visiting different places."

Christy flipped through her notebook. "Okay. Sylvia May, right?" Her hard eyes landed on Sylvia.

Sylvia blinked and nodded. She rocked her chair faster.

"You won't be taking any trips anytime soon. Come with me. I have a few questions for you."

Martha jumped up and put her arm around Sylvia's frail shoulders. "You'll be fine. Just answer Detective Crank's questions." She walked with Sylvia to the door, offering comfort for her friend of decades.

Detective Crank took Sylvia's arm. "You three stay here," she said in her no-nonsense voice.

As soon as the detective and Sylvia were out of earshot, all three women started talking at once. Annie held up her hand. "Martha, you first. You've known Sylvia forever. Is there any chance she shot Forrest?"

Martha frowned. "I can't believe you feel like you have to ask that question, Annie. Of course not. I don't believe she could hurt anything."

"She was in the office. She admits to owning a gun. She was desperate for money that just happens to be missing." Annie ticked the items off on her fingers.

"So now you're saying she stole the money *and* killed Forrest?"

Annie stood and paced across the small room. "I'm not saying that at all. I'm stating facts, and that's exactly what Christy will focus on: means, opportunity, and motive. Sylvia was in the room, she was desperate for money, and she owns a gun. I would describe her position to be precarious at best."

"If we're talking hypotheticals, *why* did she kill Forrest?" Martha asked.

"He saw her take the money?"

"Where did she hide it? Or the gun, for that matter, that she said went missing last week, let me remind you."

"Good question. If she never left the office, it would have to be in there someplace still." Annie looked out the window of the apartment. "Marvin might know more. He has that reputation of snooping around. He saw Sylvia, maybe he saw someone else."

"Maybe Marvin followed Forrest and killed him," Mia suggested.

"Okay, let's consider Marvin. Why would he kill Forrest?" Annie asked.

"Marvin said Forrest stole money from him so he wanted revenge," Martha said with a satisfied look on her face. She obviously was happy to have the conversation on anyone but her friend, Sylvia.

"Would he have used Sylvia's gun?" Mia wondered.

"First of all, we don't know if her gun is the murder weapon, but let's assume it is. Marvin could have stolen it when he was doing his sneaking around. Sylvia seems like she's an open book. Maybe she told Marvin about her gun. Maybe she even showed it to him so he would know where she kept it," Annie said. "Why on earth did she have a gun, anyway?"

Martha shrugged. "If it's the same gun her mother passed down to her, I guess she kept it for sentimental reasons. I don't even know if it still works. But I do know that Sylvia was an expert shot in her youth."

Before they could speculate any further about Sylvia, Marvin, or come up with other possible suspects, Detective Crank returned with Sylvia walking slowly behind her. Her face was drained of color and she had the look of someone who didn't know if she was coming or going.

Detective Crank, on the other hand, was almost cheerful.

"Annie? You next." Detective Crank wiggled her finger, turned around, and walked out of Sylvia's apartment without waiting to see if Annie followed or not.

Of course, she did follow. Her mind raced with the memory of the crime scene she walked into when she found Sylvia in the closet, trying to see every detail that could help get her out of trouble.

Christy opened a door next to the office where Forrest's body had been found. It was set up almost identically, with a desk, a couple of extra chairs, a lush spider plant decorating the corner of the desk, and a window overlooking the side parking lot. There was a door in the wall that was shared with the other office. She wondered if it was a closet.

"Have a seat." Christy gestured to one of the office chairs and she sat behind the desk. She steepled her fingers under her chin and stared at Annie. "Your friend told me some interesting things."

Annie scooched forward on her chair and sat up straight instead of slouching against the back. "First of all, I only met Sylvia tonight at the Easter dinner. I really don't know her."

"Tell me about the Easter dinner." Christy sat back, picked up a pen and doodled on a pad in front of her. "Did you serve ham?"

Annie scrunched her brows together. "Yes, but how is that relevant?"

"It could be. What else did you serve?"

"Appetizers before dinner. Ham with pineapple, scalloped potatoes, green beans, and rolls for dinner. Cake and ice cream for dessert. With chocolate sprinkles."

Christy closed her eyes and breathed in deeply. "Sounds delicious. I did wonder why the Easter bunny smelled like potatoes. Did he hop across the table or something?"

"He knocked a tray of the scalloped potatoes off the counter. He made quite a mess before dinner when it oozed over the floor and all over his feet." Annie tried to figure out what Christy's point was with all this talk of food.

"Any leftovers? I'm starving."

Ahhh, that was the point. "Nope. Every pan is washed and put away. Dawn, the manager, took the leftover cake. I told you that already. And a vegetarian meal went to someone who didn't come to the dining room."

"Do you know whose office this is?" Christy asked, abruptly changing the direction of her questions, a strategy that Annie was quite used to—first some small talk, and then dig into the main point of her questions.

Annie shook her head.

Christy stood. "Sylvia told me that this is the secretary's office," she glanced at her notebook, "Gloria Knight. Do you know her?"

"I met her at the dinner. We talked for a few minutes because she had a special request, a vegetarian meal. She was friendly and gave me the impression that she spends more hours working here than she would like."

"Did you notice when she left the dining room?"

"I gave her the extra vegetarian entree for one of the residents who didn't come to the dining room." Annie paused to rewind her brain. "I don't remember exactly when she left. I was kind of busy, but I think most of the seniors left before Dawn and Gloria. And before Forrest, for that matter."

Christy opened the door in the common wall. "Gloria and Dawn's offices are connected without having to go into the hallway."

Annie stood next to Christy and looked into the crime scene. "So someone could have left Dawn's office through this door. But then what? They still would have to get out of here."

Christy pointed to another door. "There is an outside door in this office. But Sylvia did admit that she was hiding in the closet next door when she heard the gunshot, which puts her at the crime scene at the time of the murder. Did you see anyone in the hallway or leaving this office when you entered Dawn's office?"

Annie closed her eyes. She had been so focused on Sylvia's urgent message that she didn't pay attention to who else was around.

"Martha, Mia, and I ran from the dining room to the door of Dawn's office after Sylvia texted that she heard the gunshot. I guess most of the seniors were in their apartments. I don't remember seeing anyone."

"And you burst right inside?"

"No, I opened the door and felt for the light switch, then peeked inside. It was quiet at first, then I heard a sob and rushed in to find Sylvia. I didn't even see Forrest's body until after I helped her out of the closet."

"And the safe?"

"The door was open with a stack of folders inside when I came into the office."

"Sylvia told me that Dawn kept quite a bit of cash inside."

Annie nodded. "She told me that, too."

"Do you know why Sylvia was even in the office?" Christy asked.

Before Annie could answer, Dawn Cross barged into the room. "What's going on here? I was home, finally, and got a call from the police that a Detective Crank had some questions for me. I'm not happy."

Annie felt the tiniest of a twinge of sympathy for Dawn when she saw Christy's lip twitch at the edges. It wasn't a twitch that would grow into a friendly smile. That was for sure. Not with her eyes darkened to a steely shade of gray as she walked toward Dawn.

"And who are *you* here in Gloria's office?" Dawn pointed at Christy. She obviously was used to running the show at Golden Living, but Annie could feel a storm brewing and settling around Dawn for a rude awakening.

Christy let her butt rest against the desk. She crossed her arms. The silence settled like a dark cloud. "Dawn Cross?"

"That's right. Who the heck are you?"

"Detective Christy Crank. I'm the one who requested your presence."

Dawn's body shrank a bit as she understood her blunder. Annie stood. "I'll leave and let you two have some privacy."

Dawn's eyes darted between Christy and Annie. "Can one of you please fill me in on what's going on? This place is over run with—"

"How about you take a seat, Ms. Cross, and let *me* ask the questions," Christy said as she pointed to a chair. "Don't leave yet, Ms. Hunter."

Christy turned her attention back to Dawn and asked, "How was the cake?"

"Sorry?" Dawn scrunched her eyebrows.

Christy nodded toward Annie. "She wrapped up the leftover cake for you to take home. I'm wondering how you enjoyed it."

"Oh, um, I forgot it in my office. I had a little distraction and, I guess, I just forgot to pick it up when I left."

Christy sat behind the desk with her chin resting on one upturned palm. She stared at Dawn. "A little distraction. What was the little distraction, if you don't mind me asking?"

"We do have a privacy policy here."

Christy slammed her hand on the desk. Both Dawn and Annie jumped. "Tell me what the distraction was, please."

"Sylvia May has some, shall I say, financial problems. She followed me into my office and kept nagging about giving her more time to pay." She leaned toward

Christy. "Listen, I have the CEOs on my back to make this place profitable and I can't give every one of these seniors a special rate once their funds get low so they don't have to move. Sylvia didn't like the answer I gave. I asked her to leave so I could finish up some business and get home."

"What business?" Christy tilted her head and kept her eyes on Dawn.

Dawn squirmed in her seat. "Writing some checks."

"Checks for who?"

"I had to pay Forrest Spring for his Easter bunny role and," she glanced at Annie, "the Black Cat Café for the dinner tonight."

"Ms. Hunter, did you get paid?"

"I did not." Annie hesitated, choosing her words carefully. "By the time I got to Ms. Cross's office, she was gone."

Christy smiled. "That is interesting. I wonder where that check is. Ms. Cross, can you explain?"

"No. This is ridiculous." She stood quickly. Her chair scraped backwards as her legs bumped against it. "I don't even know why I'm here. You ask me questions about cake, clients, and checks. I've had it up to here." Her hand waved over the top of her head.

"Sit down," Christy barked. "You want to know why you're here? Because someone was found dead in your office and I intend to get to the bottom of it."

"Dead?"

"Yes."

Fortunately, Dawn's chair was still close enough to her when her knees buckled. She landed right back where she had been. Her mouth hung open. "Dead?" she repeated again in a whisper. "Who?"

"Forrest Spring, Ms. Cross. The Easter bunny was found dead in your office. And we haven't found the check you said you wrote for him."

Christy was clever.

Annie was stunned.

Dawn fainted.

CHAPTER 6

Christy winked at Annie after she propped Dawn securely on her chair and gave her some water to sip. "Are you feeling a little better now?"

Dawn nodded.

"I have your checkbook here, and before Ms. Hunter leaves, I'd like you to pay her the balance due on the account. From everything I heard tonight, the dinner was superb, the cleanup is done, and now it's time for you to live up to your end of the bargain." Christy handed Dawn a pen.

Without any flourish, Dawn wrote the check and handed it to Annie.

"And now a check for the money you owed Mr. Easter Bunny."

"What? You told me he's dead."

"Make it out to cash and I'll be sure his next of kin gets the money."

Dawn wrote the check. "Is that why you called me down here? To twist my arm to write a couple of checks?" She stood. "I'm going home now."

Christy placed her hand on Dawn's shoulder. "Not so fast. We still have the matter of a body in your office."

Dawn fell back into the chair. "How about you tell me all about the safe in your office?"

"It's a safe. I keep stuff inside." Dawn's tone had a belligerent edge to it.

"What *exactly* do you keep inside?" Christy leaned against the desk.

Annie felt forgotten and couldn't decide if she should stand up and leave but curiosity over where this next line of questioning was headed won out and she stayed put. She sensed that Dawn was walking right into a trap.

"All the personal records of everyone who lives at Golden Living."

"Anything else?"

"No," she muttered.

Annie felt her eyebrows pitch up. No? What about the money that Sylvia had seen inside? Someone was lying.

Christy tapped her chin. "What time did you say you got home?"

"I don't think I did say."

"Right. Now you can tell me."

Dawn pursed her lips. She took a quick glance at the clock in the office. Annie could tell she was trying to calculate what the 'right' answer was as Christy waited with her foot tapping the seconds away.

"I think it was somewhere around seven."

Christy nodded. "And what time did you get to Dawn's office, Annie?"

"I was just done cleaning up and headed to the office a little before seven. I was pretty sure Dawn wouldn't have waited for me. To be honest, I was pretty annoyed with her attitude about paying the balance of the bill." Annie looked at the check she still held in her hand. "Thanks for this."

"You've got your check and you're free to leave now while I finish up with some questions for Ms. Cross. Thank you for your patience, Annie."

"How come she can leave? And what about Gloria?"

Annie paused in the doorway.

"Gloria?" Detective Crank asked in her I-have-no-idea-who-you-are-talking-about voice.

"Yeah, Gloria Knight. She's the secretary and this is her office. She's the one you should be talking to."

"Why is that, Ms. Cross?"

"She had a problem with Forrest."

"And you didn't? I was told by a reliable source that he thought you might not pay him tonight. Why was he concerned about that?"

Dawn flicked her wrist. "Just a misunderstanding."

Annie left Gloria's office. Wow, she hadn't fully processed what just happened but she was pretty sure that Detective Crank had some strong suspicions about Dawn Cross and what happened to Forrest Spring. She needed to find out all she could about that relationship.

Annie hustled down the hallway to Sylvia's apartment.

"Pssst."

Annie's head swiveled to one side. Marvin stood in the shadows.

"Dawn didn't leave when she told the detective she left."

"Marvin? Were you listening to the whole conversation?" Annie was dumbfounded. How did he get close enough without a police officer seeing him?

Marvin grinned. "There's a bathroom next to Gloria's office. Those policemen didn't pay any attention to an old man like me shuffling in to take a pee. I could hear everything through the wall."

Annie grabbed Marvin's arm. "You better come with me and tell me what else you know."

Marvin shook Annie's arm away. "I don't think so, Missy. I have my show to watch. I never miss my crime show at nine."

Nine already? Annie had expected to be home by seven-thirty at the latest. Jason would be wondering where she was. She sent a quick text to let him know she'd be home soon.

Marvin moved silently down the hall and turned into the apartment next to Sylvia's. Annie had to admit that Gloria's description of him being a creeper was right on the money. What else did he know? For that matter, did he follow Forrest into Dawn's office and kill him?

Martha peeked around the door of Sylvia's apartment. She made a circular motion with her arm, beckoning Annie inside. "Get in here and tell us what's going on."

The tea kettle whistled shrilly, giving Sylvia's apartment a cozy feel. Almost, if it wasn't for the dark cloud hovering above.

"What took so long?" Martha whispered as she filled a teapot covered with rabbits. "Chamomile to calm our nerves," she added.

Annie settled on the loveseat next to her mother with her tea. "I'm still processing the conversation, but I have to admit, Christy is clever. Dawn arrived and she never saw the train wreck she ended up in."

"Is she the murderer?" Sylvia asked.

"She has some explaining to do and Christy caught her in a lie. Dawn doesn't know it, but I'm sure it will come back to haunt her." Annie sipped the tea carefully. "Ahhh. I can feel the calmness already."

"What lie?" they all asked at the same time as they leaned toward Annie.

"About the money in the safe. Christy asked her what she kept in the safe and all she said was personal records for all the people that live here."

Sylvia jerked upright. "What personal records? She doesn't have a right to keep records on us, does she?"

Annie shrugged. "I don't know about that. I suppose it depends on what's in the records. Maybe it's just a spreadsheet about payments and things like that."

"And anytime she writes up someone for an infraction. Marvin probably has the thickest file in there for all his rule-breaking." Sylvia resumed rocking in her chair.

Annie set her cup on the small table next to the loveseat. "Speaking of Marvin, he told me that Dawn lied to Christy about what time she actually left."

"How would Marvin know?" Martha sipped her tea and helped herself to a chocolate egg in a basket placed between all the women.

"He said he listened to the conversation from the bathroom next to Gloria's office."

"Have you considered that Marvin could be the killer?" Mia asked. "He seems to know an awful lot about everyone's comings and goings tonight so he had to be in the vicinity of Dawn's office."

"It did cross my mind. He saw Sylvia go in before Forrest arrived. Did he follow Forrest in while Sylvia was hiding in the closet?" Annie finished her tea and carried her cup to Sylvia's small but efficient kitchen. "My brain is overloaded with all this information. I'm going home to relax, get a good night's sleep, and face tomorrow in a few hours."

Mia and Martha stood also. "We'll rendezvous at the Black Cat Café in the morning?" Martha asked.

"I could sure use your help with Leona gone until Friday. With Easter coming down the bunny trail, I have to stock up with lots of delicious baked goods. I'll be there bright and early."

Sylvia rinsed all the tea cups. "Thank you for keeping me company tonight. I'm not sure what that detective thought after I told her I was hiding in the closet and heard the gunshot. Do you think there's any chance she might think I'm the murderer and made up the story about hiding in the closet?"

"Detective Crank is thorough," Annie said, choosing her words carefully. "She'll look at all the facts and clues before she makes a decision."

Annie didn't want to scare Sylvia but, yes, Annie thought there was a strong chance that Christy was suspicious of Sylvia's story. And if the murder weapon turned out to be Sylvia's missing gun, that would be even worse for Sylvia. Tracking down who stole the gun, if it *was* stolen, was important. And Marvin could very well hold the key to that information.

CHAPTER 7

By the time Annie got home and told Jason the crazy events of her day, starting with Leona up and leaving on a vacation and ending with the dead Easter bunny, he suggested it might be time for her to call Leona to get home and take charge of the mess.

"No. I can't do that. Leona and my mother have complete confidence in me and I don't want to let them down." Annie stroked Roxy's soft head as her terrier lay on the couch next to her. "I need to see this through to the end."

"Well. I know you can do it. You can do anything you set your mind to."

It made Annie feel good to know that her handsome husband had confidence in her abilities, even if she doubted herself at times.

"It's just that I hate to worry about you, Annie." He scooched close to her and put his arm around her shoulders. "Please don't put yourself in any dangerous situations."

"The only danger I foresee is burning down the Black Cat Café." She laughed. "That's what pushed Leona over the edge to take a few days off."

"There was a fire at the café?"

"No, but she burned the cake for the Easter dinner. You should have been there. I can laugh about it now—cake all over the floor with other baking utensils landing in the pile." Annie tucked her feet up and twisted her body to face Jason. "I have to make this work. For Leona, and for myself, too, I guess. I need to know I can step in and take charge if she needs to get away."

Jason's fingers twisted through Annie's curls and he stared into her eyes. Shivers traveled through her body. She tucked herself into the space between his strong chest and his muscular arm, the space that she filled perfectly. "There was a vegetarian at the dinner."

"What did you make?"

"Stuffed zucchini, and it came out quite nice if I don't say so myself. I'll make it for you sometime." She closed her eyes and let her body relax. The problems of the day drifted away in the safety of Jason's arm and disappeared completely as they made their way to bed.

When the alarm screeched very early Thursday morning, the last thing Annie wanted to do was leave the toasty cocoon next to Jason. Her fingers found the snooze button but he threw the comforter off. "No going back to sleep. You have baking to do. Did you forget that you have a café to run?"

Annie groaned.

"No letting down your mother and your aunt. That's what you told me last night." Jason clapped his hands. "Chop, chop. Time to get up."

"How can you be so cheerful this early?" Annie trudged into the bathroom for a quick shower, hoping to wash away the cobwebs and get motivated for the day.

Jason snuck his hand in the shower, turned the faucet to cold, and gave Annie a shock of icy water. *That* woke her up with a shriek. "Just trying to help. Coffee will be ready by the time you're downstairs."

Annie pulled her comb through her wet hair, knowing it would do exactly what it wanted as it dried despite her best efforts to tame it. She pulled on her comfy jeans and favorite green t-shirt with a big black cat sitting with its tail wrapped around its feet. Her nose led her downstairs and straight to the source of the delicious coffee aroma.

"This new coffee-maker is fool-proof," Jason said as he handed Annie a mug of steaming-hot dark roast. "Even I can manage." He smiled. "All ready for today?"

"I'm ready to stock up the pastry display with carrot cupcakes, éclairs, cheesecakes covered with strawberries, and whatever else is on Leona's list. What I'm not ready for are the unknown disasters. Yesterday was a huge lesson for me in what it takes to run a business where so much can go wrong. My art gallery runs itself at the moment, but with the café, there's always the possibility of a food allergy, special request, not getting delivery of what you need when you need it—so much can go wrong."

"And a body doesn't help."

"That didn't have anything to do with the food, at least."

"But you were *there* because of the food," Jason said.

Annie finished her coffee, grabbed her bag and sweatshirt and plopped a kiss on Jason's cheek. "I'd better run. It doesn't look good if the boss isn't the first to arrive."

"Uh-oh." The space between Jason's eyebrows wrinkled. "You might be starting to enjoy this new position of power."

Annie laughed as she closed the door.

As she drove to the Black Cat Café, she had a lot to think about. *Did* she like being in charge? There certainly was satisfaction for a job well done, *but* dealing with all the rest was stressful at best and scary if she let herself dwell on what happened at the Golden Living retirement home.

Annie pulled into the deserted parking lot just before her mother's car parked right next to her.

"I figured I'd get here early, too, so we can get a good start before the customers start arriving. This will be another long day if we plan to get ahead of the busy weekend."

Annie turned the radio on as soon as she stowed her bag behind the counter. Leona's oldies station had become such a habit to start the day, she knew it would be a good motivator. She chose a lime green apron covered with jumping black cats, thinking the energy on the apron was a good sign, and threw a red apron with cats stalking each other to her mother.

"Any more news about the murder?" Mia asked Annie.

"Nope, just the way I like it. Christy is in charge and I plan to stay as far away as possible."

"Until someone needs your help," Mia muttered under her breath but loud enough for Annie to hear.

"Like who?" Annie got out the food processor and several pounds of carrots.

"Well, while you were being questioned by Christy last night, Martha promised Sylvia that you would help her."

"She *what*? How could she do that without asking first? What can *I* do?"

"You do have a special knack for asking questions and finding important clues. That's probably what Martha was thinking." Mia leaned against the counter. "Sylvia is worried."

"I'm not surprised." She peeled carrots aggressively. How was she supposed to keep the Black Cat Café going properly and search for clues to help Sylvia? "Do you think she told us everything that happened last night?"

"What are you thinking she may have left out?"

Annie turned on the food processor, making conversation impossible but giving her time to think. She set the shredded carrots aside and started on the batter for the cupcakes. "Where did the money go? What I'm wondering is, why did Sylvia really go into Dawn's office twice—once to talk to Dawn, but then why did she go back?"

"You probably have a theory."

Annie stirred while she explained what she was thinking. "Here's another possibility. What if Sylvia followed Dawn to her office to ask for an extension to pay her monthly expenses, or something like that, and Dawn said no? Sylvia might have decided to go back a second time to steal the money from the safe to have money to make her payment, and that's when Forrest showed up and she hid in the closet."

"Sylvia just doesn't strike me as the type to steal," Mia argued.

Annie wagged her finger at her mother. "Great point. The bottom line is—if it wasn't Sylvia, who did steal the money and where is it?"

With cupcakes going in and out of the oven and the pastry display getting filled with all the Easter offerings, Annie got lost in her own thoughts. There was something about working through all the possibilities connected to Forrest's murder that felt like solving a puzzle, but getting in Christy's way was *not* something she relished. Their hot and cold relationship always iced over if Annie ended up anywhere near Christy's investigation.

Thinking of the devil, Christy pushed through the door just as the café opened for business. "All that talk of your dessert last night made me crave some carrot cake. Got any?" she asked Mia.

"Of course. But take a look at everything else before you decide. Annie added some awesome desserts to the display this morning besides the carrot cupcakes."

Christy gazed at the pastry display and her eyes lit up at the sight of the carrot cupcakes covered with cream cheese frosting and decorated with an orange piped-on carrot. On one side of the cupcakes, Mia pointed out some individual raspberry custard tarts and on the other side, she had mini éclairs with strawberries and cream.

"And don't forget these coconut chick cupcakes or a ricotta cheesecake." Mia worked her way around the case, naming all the different desserts. "And chocolate covered strawberries."

"Stop! Now you've given me too many choices when I thought I knew exactly what I wanted," Christy complained while laughing. "You choose. Just give me a half dozen assorted and a dozen carrot cupcakes. That should keep everyone at the police station happy after their late night."

Annie's ears perked up. "Did you get to the bottom of your investigation?" She tried to make her voice sound casual.

"Nice try." Christy snatched one of the carrot cupcakes before Mia closed the box and took a big bite. "Mmm. These should be illegal," she mumbled, spraying crumbs on the counter. "Oops. Sorry." She chewed and swallowed before turning to Annie. "I do have one question for you, Annie. Did you happen to meet someone at the dinner last night by the name of Marvin Yates?"

Annie nodded. "I did have the pleasure."

"*Pleasure*? You must be thinking of someone else. There was nothing pleasurable about the Marvin I met. One of the policemen on duty caught this guy sneaking along the hallway, eavesdropping on my conversations."

"That sounds like Marvin. I was told that Dawn wrote him up for snooping around at night when everyone was supposed to be in their apartment. Gloria, the secretary, called him a creeper."

"That's a good description." Christy finished the cupcake.

"Is he a suspect?" Annie arranged several colorful marshmallow Easter critters on a tray.

"Of course. Everyone who was in the building is a suspect, although we've eliminated many that had verifiable alibis."

"Dawn was pretty uncomfortable when you were questioning her while I was still there with you." Annie wanted to get as much information from Christy as possible but she couldn't be direct or the detective would clam up.

"Yeah, she has some holes in her story. I can't verify the time she said she left or the time she said she got home."

That was an interesting tidbit of information. Annie wondered if Marvin had those details—or at least when she left Golden Living. From what she gathered, it didn't sound like he missed much.

Not long after Christy left with her two boxes of goodies, Martha walked into the café with two unexpected customers.

CHAPTER 8

"Go ahead and sit over at that booth and I'll bring you both some coffee." Annie watched silently as Martha pointed to an empty booth with a view overlooking Heron Lake.

"I'll get my own coffee. I don't want anyone touching something I put in my mouth," Marvin said as he moved away from Martha and picked up a mug from the drink cart. He inspected the mug carefully, rejected it, and took another that was all the way in the back. He leaned close to each label describing the different types of coffees and chose the hazelnut blend. "Is this real whipped cream? Golden Living never gives us real whipped cream. I should just cook my own food instead of paying for their mushy meals."

"Yes, Marvin. I whipped it this morning," Mia assured him.

He added an extra-large helping of whipped cream, stuck a cinnamon stick in his coffee, and carried it to the booth. He slid on the opposite side from Sylvia who waited patiently for Martha to deliver her coffee.

"Just regular for me, please," Sylvia said after she took a look at Marvin's mug.

Martha carried two coffees to the booth and slid in next to Sylvia. Annie followed closely behind her with a tray of pastries. "On the house," Annie assured them.

Marvin quickly snatched a raspberry custard tart before the tray even hit the table or Sylvia had a chance to see what was on the tray. She sat staring out the window instead of enjoying her coffee or a pastry.

"Come on now, Sylvia, you've got to eat something. I thought if I got you away from that building with those bad memories you'd be able to relax a little." Martha pushed Sylvia's coffee closer and placed a mini éclair with strawberries and cream on a napkin next to the mug. "Try this. One bite and you won't be able to resist eating the whole thing."

Annie wanted to stay and listen to the conversation. She knew it wasn't luck that brought Sylvia and Marvin in this morning. Martha planned to get as much information from them as possible, Annie suspected, and she wouldn't mind if she crashed their party.

Martha helped herself to a carrot cupcake. "My favorite. Annie," she said. "Don't tell Leona I said this, but these are better than anything she ever made."

Annie felt a glowing bit of pride but knew Martha was exaggerating. "Don't worry. I definitely won't tell her, especially after she burned her cake and I had to start over from scratch."

Martha raised her eyebrows. "I bet Leona doesn't want *that* bit of news to get around. Do you have time to sit with us for a minute?" She asked before Annie could turn and go back to the kitchen.

The sweets wouldn't bake themselves. They were perilously low on the Black Cat Café's signature sweet—blueberry muffins. Annie glanced at the clock and decided she could spare a few minutes for a break before whipping up a batch. She fixed herself a cup of coffee and sat next to Marvin. He slid closer to the window, pulling his napkin with the rest of his tart along with him.

"How are you doing today, Sylvia?" Annie asked, trying her best to ignore Marvin's weirdness.

Sylvia's shoulders rose and fell with a big intake and exhale of air. "I just don't know what to do. That detective was so nice, but I'm afraid I may have told her more than I should have."

"Nice? I wouldn't use that word to describe her," Marvin said. "She kept trying to trick me. Just like everyone else. Dawn, my kids, and now that detective." Marvin carefully folded the napkin out of the way and nibbled a corner of the tart.

Annie added paranoid to her list of descriptions for Marvin. "How did Detective Crank try to trick you?"

"She wanted to know where I went after I left the dining room. I told her it was none of her business."

"I bet that went over well." Annie chuckled. "If you didn't give her an alibi, she'll have you on the suspect list. Did you think of that?"

Marvin considered what Annie said, then took another bite. "That's ridiculous. Dawn lied to the detective. She's the one who killed Forrest. You know what I think? Dawn hired him to be the Easter bunny so she could get rid of him before he had a chance to rat her out about the money."

"The money. The money in the safe?" Annie asked Marvin. He spoke with such certainty but, of course, he might just be making everything up.

Marvin finished the tart and licked the cream off his cinnamon stick before he drank a little. "Is this your place?" he asked Annie.

"No. It belongs to my aunt but she took a few days off. Is your coffee okay?"

"Better than the coffee at Golden Living, but that doesn't mean much." He drank a little more, then returned to his earlier thoughts. "Dawn steals the money from all of us. You," he pointed to Sylvia. "Why do you think you might have to move?"

"You mean she's taking more than she should?"

"That's exactly what I mean. She's doing the same thing to me. I told my kids I wanted to go back to my house and my little dog. Get out of the joke called Golden Living, but they said Golden Living owns my house now. I call that stealing. I saw all that cash in her safe but she keeps a tight watch over it."

Annie actually felt a twinge of sorrow listening to Marvin. She thought his kids might have sold the house so he could stay at Golden Living, but did they do it behind his back? "Where is your dog now?"

"Scout? He's with my son. I petitioned to have him move in with me, and Dawn said okay until I actually moved in, then it was 'sorry, we've changed the policy and no animals are allowed,'" he said in a sicky-sweet-sing-song voice.

Martha reached across the table and covered Marvin's hand with her own. "That's terrible. Let's just break the rule."

Marvin's eyes lit up like an excited kid. "How? My son will never bring Scout over. He doesn't want me to get kicked out. And, believe me, I've been trying."

"Annie? How about bringing Roxy over for a little visit?" Martha suggested.

Marvin twisted on the seat. "You have a dog? You could bring her in through my window. That's what I tried to get my son to do, but he's not a rule breaker. Will you do it?"

Annie was startled by Marvin's faded blue eyes with such a passionate plea. She hadn't really looked beyond his quirks, but now she saw his neatly pressed button-down shirt, carefully combed thick white hair, and his unwavering gaze.

What was Annie getting herself involved in? She should be spending the afternoon baking to get farther ahead for the weekend. But, on the other hand, it might be the only way to get Marvin to open up about his discoveries from all his snooping. That money had to be somewhere. And what about Sylvia's gun? Christy didn't want Annie to get in the way of her investigation but she couldn't say Annie wasn't allowed to visit her new friends at Golden Living.

Three sets of eyes were focused on her face, waiting for an answer. Martha, who had helped Annie in so many ways since she returned to Catfish Cove. Sylvia and Marvin who had no one else watching out for their interests and now seemed to be putting all their hopes on Annie.

"Okay. I'll bring Roxy over for a quick visit later this afternoon; after I close up for the day. It will be the perfect outing for her with her newly completed therapy dog training."

Marvin's eyes blinked and Annie was sure she saw tears about to spill out. She started to slide out of the seat but Marvin touched her arm.

"I can't wait. Thank you."

One thing about Marvin, Annie decided, was that he had a huge heart for animals and that made him a decent person in her book. Maybe his gruffness toward the people in his life at the moment was warranted, she would hold off judgement on that for now. "I need to get back to work."

From behind the counter, Annie's eyes followed the three elderly people as they left the café. She couldn't help but wonder if both Sylvia and Marvin had simply been in the wrong place at the wrong time after the Easter dinner, or were they hiding secrets that could be Annie's undoing?

The rest of the day flew by between serving customers, baking, and trying *not* to think too much about what she had agreed to do. If only she could be in two places at the same time, she could keep her obligation to Leona *and* help Sylvia and Marvin. That would be the answer to her problem.

At four, Annie locked up the café. She walked outside with her mother and they both stopped to enjoy the late afternoon sunshine.

"Leona will be proud of how hard you're working while she's gone," Mia said as she gave her daughter a quick hug.

"Working hard isn't the problem, it's juggling all the unexpected problems that pop up all day." Annie sighed. At least the peaceful view helped settle her adrenaline-charged body. Mixing, baking, making pleasant chit chat with customers, all while letting the events of the night before run in the background kept her brain buzzing.

"You had a conversation with Martha, Sylvia, and Marvin," Mia said, not as a question, but Annie could tell she hoped to hear the details.

"Marvin thinks Dawn Cross is stealing money from all the seniors renting at Golden Living."

"He is an odd duck. What do *you* think?"

"I think I need to find out more about what's going on."

"I was afraid you'd say that. Even with all the extra responsibility here, you have time to get involved with the murder?" Annie felt Mia's eyes on her but she kept her focus on the lake. The gentle repetitive lapping at the water's edge was soothing.

Annie thought through her answer before responding. "It's not a question of having the time, it's more about doing what I feel in my heart is the right thing to do. When Marvin actually looked at me with a sad desperation in his eyes, I knew I couldn't say no to at least try to help get to the bottom of what Dawn might be up to." She suddenly turned and looked at her mother. "What if she *is* stealing from those people? Someone needs to consider that possibility. Don't worry, I'm not going to do anything heroic, just make a visit with Roxy."

"You think Roxy will sniff out the missing money?" Mia said with definite sarcasm in her tone.

"Not exactly. Roxy is my in with Marvin. He misses his dog and he knows what's going on at Golden Living. Maybe Roxy will help him trust me enough to share more information. That's all."

"And you'll pass that on to Detective Crank?"

"If there's anything to pass on, of course I will," Annie said with more confidence than she felt. She knew Detective Crank tolerated her at best and would ridicule her at the first chance possible. Marvin Yates wasn't the most believable witness with his stories that sounded more like a conspiracy theory than a plausible scenario.

CHAPTER 9

When Annie arrived home to Cobblestone Cottage, the pull to kick off her shoes, enjoy a cold drink on the porch, and watch the world go by almost derailed her promise to Marvin. But Roxy's enthusiastic, full-body-wiggle greeting reminded her that Marvin didn't have a loyal dog where he was now living.

She patted Roxy's head. "Ready for an adventure?"

Roxy's tail thumped against one side, then the other, showing her always present enthusiasm for anything.

"Let me find your therapy dog coat. I have no intention of sneaking you inside through a window. We'll be walking right through the front door so we can guilt Dawn Cross into welcoming us with open arms." At least, Annie told herself, that's how she *hoped* it would go.

When Annie arrived at the retirement home, she wasn't so distracted with delivering the catered dinner and noticed more details about the place. The circular drive leading to the front was immaculately landscaped and welcoming. Although it was a large sprawling building, the dark green siding with cream trim felt homey. With a small visitor parking area in front and a larger area on the right side, Annie chose to park out of the way on the side. She assumed that was where employees parked, using the side entrance instead of the main one.

Annie let Roxy sniff outside for a few minutes before she led the way to the front door. As soon as they entered, Gloria stopped dead in her tracks to look at Roxy. "What a handsome dog. I thought I was seeing the ghost of a terrier I had when I was a kid." She crouched down to Roxy's level.

That was a promising sign for their visit. "This is Roxy, my therapy dog. I had a request from Sylvia May for a visit? I'm sure, considering what she went through yesterday, there won't be any problems."

"Oh, I didn't recognize you at first. You catered the dinner." Gloria stood. "Your stuffed zucchini was delicious. I'd love to have the recipe, unless it's a trade secret."

"Of course. I'll be sure to get it to you." Annie began walking in the direction of Sylvia's apartment. "I know the way."

"I suppose I should check with Dawn first. She insists on approving all visitors." Gloria rolled her eyes to show she thought it was a ridiculous policy. "How about you wait right here. I'll only be a minute." Gloria's heels click-clacked down the hall.

"Should we bother waiting, Roxy? I really don't care if she approves our visit. I think I can bluff my way out of any issues with your therapy dog status." Annie continued toward Gloria's office but suddenly stopped before the door when she overheard Gloria say her name.

"Annie Hunter is here... What harm can it do to let her visit with Sylvia? That poor woman has enough on her plate with her worries about finding someplace else to live...Great, bye."

Who was Gloria on the phone talking to? Dawn? Annie knocked on the door. "Am I all cleared to make my visit?"

Gloria smiled, nodded, and waved her on her way.

The visitor bathroom caught Annie's attention and she made a quick stop. It was the same bathroom Marvin would have used the previous night when he listened in on Detective Christy Crank's interviews. "Just curious, Roxy. Maybe I can hear something through this wall."

Sure enough, as Annie stood near the wall, and Roxy sniffed every inch of the bathroom, she heard a phone ring. Gloria's voice came through, muted but clear. "Don't ever call me while I'm at work. If Dawn connects you to me, she'll never let you move in when there's an opening."

Annie frowned. Who was on the phone? At any rate, there was some kind of rivalry between Gloria and Dawn, with Gloria lower in the pecking order. She pulled the bathroom door open and almost bumped into Gloria. "Oh, sorry. Just making a pit stop before I get to Sylvia's apartment." Did that sound as lame to Gloria as it sounded to Annie's ears?

"I'll walk with you," Gloria said.

"This is a lovely facility. Do you have a waiting list for apartments?" Annie asked, hoping her question didn't ring any alarms in Gloria's head.

"There is a waiting list. Do you have someone in mind looking for a retirement home? I could get you a brochure with all the information."

"Actually, that would be great. I have an elderly neighbor and I don't know how long she'll be able to stay in her own home." Annie was thinking about Thelma Dodd who lived a few houses away from Annie and Jason. Thelma had never said anything about moving, but it was a good excuse to get the information. And look as innocent as possible.

"Stop in my office on your way out and I'll have a packet ready for you." She paused and Annie stopped next to her. "This is a sensitive question and I hope you don't take it the wrong way, but does your friend own her house?"

A big red flag waved in Annie's brain with that 'sensitive' question. Was that how this place operated? Get an elderly person to sign their house over in exchange for moving in and then kick them out saying the money was gone? "You know, I'm not sure."

Gloria patted Annie's arm. "That's okay. It's something Dawn would work with your friend on if she is interested. I try to stay out of the money aspect." She leaned close to Annie. "It can be very emotional at times."

"And the waiting list is long?"

"Well, sometimes people put their name on the list, then find a different living arrangement before a spot opens, so it's hard to say what the competition is. And sometimes, someone just can't afford it here." Gloria knocked on Sylvia's door. "Here you are. Enjoy your visit." Gloria's heels click-clacked on the tiles back the way they had come.

Martha opened the door. "I thought maybe you forgot." She pulled Annie inside. "Sylvia is a mess. That witch Dawn Cross told her she has to move out at the end of the month. She's behind on her monthly expenses and has no idea what she'll do. See what you and Roxy can do to cheer her up while I get Marvin."

Annie unclipped Roxy's leash. It only took the dog two seconds to sit next to Sylvia and place her head in Sylvia's lap. Just like when Annie visited Thelma Dodd. It was obvious that Roxy could sense when someone needed comforting; and she had an extra big soft spot for the elderly.

Martha returned with Marvin who apparently had something besides Roxy on his mind. "Did you bring any of those pastries?"

Annie chuckled at his question.

"As a matter of fact…" Annie pulled a Black Cat Café bag from her tote and handed it to Marvin. "I brought fresh-from-the-oven blueberry muffins." Well, fresh from the oven as of bright and early in the morning, but who was going to complain?

He unfolded the top of the bag and stuck his nose inside. "Do they taste as delicious as they smell?"

"Probably not," Annie teased. "I don't think you will like them." She reached over to take the bag back.

Marvin's face crunched together into a mass of wrinkled skin before a grin blossomed on his face. "You're not so bad after all." He reached in and daintily extracted a muffin. After one small nibble, his eyes closed and he sighed with satisfaction. "Better than they smell."

Annie smiled with what she felt was a huge compliment from this normally cranky man.

Martha took the bag from Marvin. "Don't hog them all. Annie brought them for all of us." She offered the open bag to Sylvia, who hesitated but ended up helping herself.

Roxy waited patiently next to Sylvia whose hand never left the terrier's head.

With everyone comfortable in Sylvia's small apartment enjoying the blueberry muffins, Martha asked, "What's the next step, Annie?"

Annie ran her fingers through her curls. "Next step?"

"Yeah, to help Sylvia keep her apartment *and* get off the suspect list," Martha said with an I-know-you-can-help tone.

Marvin finished his muffin and held his hand out toward Roxy. "Don't hog the dog, Sylvia."

Roxy looked at Annie, who sat next to Marvin, for a hint of what was expected next. Annie patted her knee and Roxy moved to her new spot within reach of Marvin's hand. His fingers stroked her ears, finding the sensitive spot that she loved and she tilted her head to make it easier for Marvin's fingers.

"How'd you get her past the warden?" Marvin asked.

"We just walked in like we belonged here. Gloria checked with Dawn and our visit was approved," Annie continued. "Marvin, you mentioned that Golden Living now owns your house. Is that the normal method for people to finance living here?"

He shrugged. "Don't know, but if we go down to the sunroom, you can talk to some other people and find out more. If they'll talk to you. There's only about a half hour before dinner so we better get a move on."

"They might not talk to me, but I bet they'll talk to Roxy. She has that effect on people." Annie stood. "Lead the way."

The sunroom was at the end of the hallway, past several apartments on that wing. The setting sun streamed through the large windows and sky lights, giving a warm, cozy setting. Large tropical plants decorated the corners, and blooming orchids filled several windows.

People sat reading or in small groups talking and playing board games. The silence when Annie and Roxy entered felt awkward and she knew her first impression would make or break the visit.

She didn't have to worry. As soon as it registered that a dog was in in the room, several people competed for Roxy's attention. This was a therapy dog's dream.

Annie walked with Roxy around the room, introducing her to the men and women who eyed Roxy with a yearning. Annie's gut instinct told her that many here missed their own pets and Roxy magically filled a tiny part of the hole in their hearts.

"What a wonderful surprise," Annie heard over and over again. "Will you come back?"

Annie had no choice but to promise more visits, not that she minded, but it would be difficult to find time in her busy schedule. She *would* find the time, one way or another.

Annie whispered to Martha, "Who's that guy sitting in the corner? He hasn't taken his eyes off me but he also doesn't look like he's approachable."

"Ask Marvin. He knows plenty about everyone."

Marvin reached for Roxy's leash. "Would it be okay if I walk with her?"

"Of course." Annie stayed with Marvin while he led Roxy to visit with more people. She waited a little while before she asked him, "Who's the guy sitting in the corner? He's making my skin crawl."

Marvin didn't even look in the direction that Annie indicated. "Sitting in a wheelchair? That's Shady Sean. He sits in that corner and scowls. He used to talk to Forrest though. I never figured out what those two had in common."

"I don't remember seeing him at the Easter dinner last night." Annie remembered Gloria telling her that he ate alone.

"He doesn't go to the dining room. Sometimes Gloria or Dawn delivers his meal. He comes in here and always sits in the same spot but never talks to anyone unless he has an insult to deliver."

"You know a lot about what goes on in this place. Will you share some of that information with me?"

When Marvin stopped walking, Roxy sat next to him. "You can ask anything you want as long as you come back with Roxy. I'll decide if I want to answer."

Annie heard footsteps approaching before she heard the voice. "What are you doing here, Annie Hunter?" Detective Christy Crank stood with her hands on her hips, staring at Annie. "I'm not sure I understand your sudden interest in Golden Living." Christy pulled Annie out of the sunroom, away from listening ears.

"Sylvia May needed some time with Roxy, my therapy dog," Annie hoped Christy bought her explanation.

Christy's carefully plucked eyebrows shot up. "Since when did Roxy become a therapy dog?"

"Recently. It's a program we've been working on."

"I'll buy that for now, but it doesn't explain why you're in *here*," Christy's arm swept around the room, "with all these other people. I don't even see Sylvia."

Annie was quite sure Christy would put two and two together expecting to figure out *why* Annie was mingling with a big group of Golden Living residents. But Annie doubted that Christy cared much about *how* Golden Living was run which, as far as Annie was concerned, was just as important as *who* killed Forrest Spring. And the *how* might very well lead to the *who*.

"Sylvia invited Marvin to visit with Roxy in her apartment and Marvin thought there were other people who would benefit from her visit. He was right. I've already promised this group that we'd be happy to come back. I suspect that many of these people miss their pets more than their families." Annie knew that Christy was a dog person and wouldn't argue with that point.

"Is that right? You're coming back. What a big surprise." The sarcasm in her tone was unmistakable. Christy leaned right next to Annie's ear. So close Annie could feel Christy's warm breath on her neck. "Don't get in my way. Don't snoop around where you don't belong. Come with your therapy dog but don't start looking for clues about the Easter bunny's murder. Understand?"

"Roxy and I will be here to help my friends through this difficult time. Do you understand how traumatic it is for them that the Easter bunny was murdered practically on their doorstep?"

"Of course I do," Christy snapped. "Don't be blinded by these hand wringing *friends* of yours. One of them could very well be the killer and no amount of you and your therapy dog will be able to help when I uncover the truth."

Annie steamed. Which friends was she referring to—Sylvia and Marvin? With a smile pasted on her face as people walked by headed to the dining room, she said goodbye and promised again to bring Roxy back.

On the way to the front door, Annie made a detour into the bathroom next to Gloria's office on the off chance of hearing more conversation. Everything was quiet. When she tried to flush the toilet, the lever wouldn't budge. Annie lifted the cover off the tank to see if it was a simple problem that she could fix.

She found the problem all right, but it wasn't simple.

Some white fuzzy clumps floated in the water above the last thing she expected to see.

She leaned against the wall and rubbed the back of her neck as her chest tightened.

She chewed on her fingernail as she tried to figure out what to do next.

She looked in the tank a second time hoping her eyes had deceived her.

No. The worst-case scenario stared back at her.

A gun rested on top of the flapper.

"What should I do, Roxy?"

There was really only one option.

She had to find Martha.

CHAPTER 10

After Annie pushed the gun off the flapper so she could flush, she replaced the toilet tank's top. She peeked out the bathroom door, her heart still in her throat. The hallway was quiet.

Annie texted Martha. *I need some help.*

While she waited, she removed the top again and took a photo. What she wanted to know was, did the gun belong to Sylvia?

Where are you? Came back from Martha.

Visitor's bathroom. Hurry.

Annie chuckled when she realized what kind of emergency Martha might be expecting to find. She heard a tap on the door. "Annie?" Martha's voice whispered. "Are you all right?"

Annie opened the door and pulled Martha inside. "Take a look at what I found." She pointed to the toilet tank.

Martha looked at Annie, scrunched her nose, and then bent forward to peer inside. Her jaw fell. "Whose is it? And what's that white stuff in the water?"

"I don't know. Did you ever see Sylvia's gun?"

"It might be hers." Martha straightened. "What are you going to do now?"

"Is Christy still in the building?"

"Yes. Can't we just take it and get rid of it?" Martha obviously thought protecting Sylvia was the only option.

Annie shook her head. "That's a really bad idea. If it is Sylvia's gun, and if she killed Forrest, we can't protect her."

"Sylvia can't be the murderer. She was hiding in the closet when she heard the gunshot, and she was still in there when you found her, so how would she have gotten rid of it in here?"

"Yes, I thought of that, too." Annie called Christy's number. She didn't even bother to say hello. "I've got something to show you. Meet me outside Gloria's office."

Annie, Martha, and Roxy filed out of the bathroom, getting a strange look from Dawn as she happened to walk by. "You're still here? Your dog couldn't wait until she got outside?"

"Yeah, something like that," Annie replied. "In case you haven't heard, our visit was a big success. There were lots of requests for a return appearance."

"So I heard. I'll agree to one more visit." Dawn turned on her heel and disappeared into Gloria's office. Dawn's office was still off-limits with yellow police tape across the door and a policeman standing outside.

Detective Crank rounded the corner. Her face was tight, her gait was fast, and her hands were clenched at her sides. Annie anticipated a barrage of comments before one word was uttered.

"This better be good." Christy halted mere inches from Annie.

"I found something in the bathroom."

Christy sighed. "I hope this isn't some kind of sick joke." She followed Annie through the door. Martha stayed in the hall with Roxy.

The toilet tank's top was still off. Annie pointed. "I don't think something like that is normally part of the plumbing."

Christy bent over the tank. "A gun? How'd it get in here?" She swiveled her head to face Annie.

"I wish I knew the answer to that question, but if you want my *opinion*—"

Christy put her hand up. "No thanks. Do you know who the gun belongs to?"

Annie shook her head. "Have you found the murder weapon yet?" Annie asked with a minute hope that Christy would answer yes and make *this* gun a moot point.

"I think we are probably looking at it." Christy pushed Annie out of the bathroom. She waved a policeman over and told him to guard the door. "No one in here. Understand?"

He nodded.

"What are you two gawking at?" Christy asked Annie and Martha. She flicked both hands, gesturing for them to get a move on.

Annie nudged Martha's arm. "Come on. I have a question for Gloria." She walked through the next door and into her office.

Dawn and Gloria were in a quiet argument. "She's got to go at the end of the month," Dawn said. "No more excuses."

Annie cleared her throat. "Excuse me. I'm here to pick up the folder about Golden Living for my friend."

Dawn's face softened into a warm smile at the mention of a possible new resident. "Did you know about this, Gloria?"

Gloria nodded, but Annie didn't miss the clenched jaw. Interesting. Why didn't she want Dawn to know?

Annie quickly glanced over her shoulder before she stepped closer to both women and cupped her hand around her mouth. "I think Detective Crank just found the murder weapon."

Color drained from both women's faces and their eyes popped open wide. "Where?" Gloria asked.

"I don't think I'm allowed to say, but I think this will move the investigation along quickly." Annie studied both women closely. Their expressions conveyed shock but Dawn's eyes shifted to the door that separated the two offices. Gloria rubbed the back of her neck.

"Before I leave," Annie began, "how do most people pay for their apartment here? I want to give as much information as possible to my friend." She smiled and tilted her head.

"There are many payment options which we can discuss with your friend," Dawn said. "Most people like to pay up front."

"Oh. How does that work since they can't possibly know how long they will need to live here?" She squinted her eyes.

"That's true, but we give a much better deal."

Annie nodded even though it explained absolutely nothing except the possibility of a scam in the works. She decided to leave it at that for now and not push her luck with too many questions. She didn't want to arouse Dawn's suspicions. She tapped the folder against her leg. "Thank you."

Martha had placed herself close enough to the door so she could hear the conversation. "I can't believe you told them about the gun."

Annie laughed. "Give them something to worry about. There's a lot more going on here than meets the eye."

"What do you mean?" Martha walked quickly to keep up with Annie. Roxy was ahead of them both, leading them back outside as quickly as possible.

Once they were outside, away from any possible snoops, Annie explained. "I think there's something fishy about how Golden Living gets paid for the apartments. Maybe not from everybody, but from some people. Now I'm wondering if Forrest was in on some kind of scam and whoever he was working with didn't want to cut him in on his share."

Martha held onto Annie's arm. "You're kidding. How did you figure all that out?"

"It's just a theory. But, Forrest did visit with a lot of the residents here so that would give him the opportunity to dig around for information about financial matters. He could have channeled that information to whoever was the mastermind, possibly with access to personal finances. Once that person had enough information, maybe it was goodbye Forrest. The problem is, I need to find some evidence before Christy will even listen to me. So, I'll have to keep digging."

"How will you manage that *and* run the café?"

Annie opened the back door of her car and let Roxy jump in. "Leona is coming back tomorrow. She won't be happy that I'll need to take some time off right before a busy weekend, but she'll understand." I hope, Annie added to herself. Annie felt sick that she would have to disappoint Leona, but who could have predicted this turn of events?

Jason wasn't home when Annie got there so she decided to take Roxy for a walk on the Lake Trail. Roxy darted back and forth, sniffing scents that were exciting for her while Annie fell into a comfortable pace. Walking usually helped clear her mind; but she couldn't clear out all the questions that popped up with no answers.

After a brisk thirty minute walk, Annie whistled for Roxy and they headed back toward Cobblestone Cottage. A steady breeze blew across the lake, whipping her curls into her face. Roxy darted up the path to Thelma Dodd's house and Annie followed.

She knocked on the door and waited for the familiar tapping of Thelma's walker.

Silence.

Annie tested the doorknob and when it turned in her hand, she pushed the door open a tiny bit. "Thelma?"

Silence.

Annie's heart raced. Roxy pushed through the door and darted toward the screened-in porch where Thelma usually sat when the weather was warm enough.

Roxy whined. She nose-butted Thelma's hand. The crossword puzzle laying in her lap slipped to the floor. Annie knelt next to Thelma's chair and gently picked up her hand. "Thelma?"

Thelma's eyes fluttered open. It took a half dozen blinks before recognition registered and she smiled. "Annie. Did you stop by for some tea?"

Annie let herself breathe again. "Do you want some?"

"That would be nice. I think I must have dozed off for a few minutes."

Annie busied herself in Thelma's kitchen fixing two cups of mint tea and she added a dog biscuit to the tray for Roxy.

With the tray on the table next to Thelma, Annie handed one cup to her. "Here you go. Are you feeling okay?"

Thelma laughed. "Yes, dear. I take my little snooze in the afternoon and feel quite refreshed afterwards." She held the dog bone out for Roxy who very gently took the treat. Thelma patted her head. "Such a well-mannered dog."

Annie picked up the crossword puzzle and was happy to see that most of the squares were filled in. She folded it carefully and placed it next to the tray.

"I haven't seen you for a while. Have you been busy?" Thelma asked as she stroked Roxy's head.

A twinge of guilt pricked at Annie's heart. She gave herself a mental reminder to bring some carrot cake cupcakes to Thelma before Easter. "I have been busy. Leona took a few days off and I feel like I've been running around like a four-year-old at an Easter egg hunt."

Thelma laughed, then her face grew serious. "I read about that poor young man who was murdered at Golden Living. What was his name?"

"Forrest Spring. I had just met him at the dinner I catered. As a matter of fact, I took Roxy to Golden Living today in her therapy dog capacity to comfort some of the residents."

"I know a few of the people that live there." Thelma sipped her tea.

Annie's ears pricked up. Of course she would know people there. Thelma had been a school teacher and she lived in Catfish Cove her whole life. Annie didn't share the fact that she used Thelma as an excuse to pick up an information folder. She was quite sure that Thelma had no intention of leaving her lakeside house.

"I know Sylvia May and Sean Woodman. Not well anymore, mind you, and I haven't seen them in ages." Thelma stared into the distance, probably reliving some long-ago memory.

"Sean Woodman? I saw a Sean today but I didn't catch his last name." Shady Sean, how Marvin called him, didn't sound like any acquaintance for Thelma in Annie's opinion. "Is he wheelchair-bound by any chance?"

"Yes, that would be Seany. Oh, he was a trouble maker, that one. Always had some kind of scheme planned. I have to admit, I had a bit of a crush on him. A very long time ago."

"Huh, he looked miserable when I saw him. And another resident told me he sits in the same corner by himself, doesn't eat in the dining room or really interact much. What happened to him?"

"It was very sad, really. He was with his father who was raising him when they were in a car crash. His father died and poor Seany was passed around from one relative to another. He was paralyzed and had a lot of anger, of course. No one could connect with him. I always wondered if he would slip off the deep end and do something horrible." Thelma lapsed back into her memories.

The hairs on Annie's neck rose.

She cleaned up the tea cups, covered Thelma's legs with a light crocheted blanket, and left with Roxy.

For the short walk to Cobblestone Cottage, Annie wondered if Thelma's words about Sean Woodman rang truer than she imagined. Did he fall off the deep end and kill Forrest Spring?

But why?

CHAPTER 11

Friday started for Annie well before the sun was out of its bed. A soft rain splashed against the windows which made the darkness feel even thicker. Roxy didn't bother to jump off the bottom corner of the bed when Annie slipped her feet to the floor.

"Jason?" she whispered.

A snore answered. She sighed. This was what Leona faced every day. No wonder she took a break. At least she would be back today.

Annie quietly tiptoed down the stairs. At least Smokey and Snowball managed to uncurl themselves to say good morning. She dumped dry food in their bowls as they wound themselves around her legs and meowed their thanks for the morning treat.

"You two would be good company at Golden Living. I'll see if I can make that happen," she said before she left Jason a note, shrugged into a light rain jacket, grabbed her tote, and silently closed the door.

The good thing about starting the day early was the peace and quiet. The bad thing was the feeling that there was someone out there watching her movements in all the stillness. She knew it was an unfounded fear, but she tensed with every shadow and shaking branch.

After she hurried inside the Black Cat Café, Annie turned on all the lights and the radio. The comforting oldies that streamed through the air helped to calm her nerves. How did Leona do it? Every day, in the dark and quiet, did it spook her, too?

Annie tied on a lime green apron with cats swatting at butterflies and pulled her supplies onto the counter—bowls, measuring cups, mixer, along with the ingredients for the morning baking. Blueberry muffins, of course, more carrot cake cupcakes, and a special order for two Easter basket cakes, one chocolate and one vanilla. That was just for starters.

Once Annie got started, focusing on the baking consumed her mind. She was finally able to forget about Forrest's murder for a few minutes. At first, a loud knocking sounded like part of the song on the radio, until it continued when the song ended.

It was only six and she didn't expect Mia to arrive until six-thirty. Being alone in the café suddenly made her heart pound. With clammy hands, she picked up her cherry rolling pin, held it in front of herself, and walked to the door.

"Annie? Are you inside?" a familiar voice asked.

Annie opened the door.

He took one look at her 'weapon' and grinned. "Do you have plans for that thing besides using it on some pastry dough?" Chief of Police, Tyler Johnson asked.

She felt foolish with the rolling pin in her hand and felt heat rise in her cheeks. "You never know." She tried to sound brave as she shrugged off his comment.

Tyler walked past Annie. "Mind if I come in?"

Since he was already inside, she assumed he didn't really expect an answer but a 'yes I do mind' almost slipped off her tongue. She *did* want to find out what he was even there for, though. Annie knew Tyler well since they had been engaged years earlier and she suspected that Christy, who played the bad cop part of the team, sent Tyler to play the good cop.

"I think that's a moot question, Tyler." She didn't even try to mask her annoyance at him interrupting her morning. "I am really busy with Leona gone and Easter right around the corner." She held the door open, hoping he might get the message that he was welcome to leave as soon as possible.

"Close the door, Annie. We need to talk." Tyler walked to the drink cart but the coffee pot was cold and empty. "No coffee yet?"

"Since you've interrupted my baking, I'll get some going. I could use it too." She busied herself with measuring the coffee and water while Tyler examined what was still in the pastry display from the day before.

"Could I bother you to get me one of those tart things? They look tasty."

The coffee machine started its magic and the rich fragrant aroma of fresh coffee filled the café. The tension that arrived at the café with Tyler's appearance slowly started to leave Annie's shoulders. She put a strawberry tart on a plate for Tyler and a mini éclair on another plate for herself.

"Get your coffee and I'll give you five minutes before I have to get back to my baking." She fixed herself a cup and sat down in front of her éclair.

Tyler did the same, sliding in across from Annie. He bit into the tart and rolled his eyes to the ceiling. "Delicious. Better than Leona's by a mile."

Annie felt the corner of her mouth twitch. "I doubt it, but thanks for the compliment." She sipped her coffee and leaned back in the booth. "What's on your mind, Tyler? I'm sure you're much too busy to just stop in for a coffee klatch."

He tilted his head and his eyes traveled over Annie's face. "I'm worried about you with this murder at Golden Living. Christy told me you were there again yesterday."

"With Roxy," Annie quickly added. "Didn't the detective tell you I went with Roxy, who is now a certified therapy dog, to visit with the people at Golden Living? They love her visits."

"Yes, Christy did mention that. And she also told me you found the murder weapon." Tyler ate the rest of the tart and eyed the éclair half still on Annie's plate. She shoved it across the table for him. Her appetite vanished as quickly as his tart disappeared with the suspense of where Tyler's conversation was headed.

It was interesting that Tyler confirmed the gun as the murder weapon. Was that a slip on his part? "What's that supposed to mean? Should I *not* have shown it to her?"

"Of course you did the right thing, but the question is—how did you know it was in the toilet tank to begin with? That's not exactly where most people would be looking for something. Who told you to check in there? Your friend, Sylvia? After all, it *is* her gun."

Annie felt her jaw drop. "I can't believe what's coming out of your mouth, Tyler Johnson." She slid out of the booth. "I think it's time for you to leave." Her whole body trembled with fury. She walked to the café door and yanked it open. "For your information, I tried to flush the toilet, and the lever wouldn't budge. Is it such a stretch to think that someone like me might lift off the top of the tank to see what the problem could be?"

"Oh." The wind was gone from his tone. "Well, stay away from Golden Living unless you want to end up as part of the investigation."

Annie *did* notice a sadness in Tyler's eyes as he looked at her on his way out. She slammed the door and kicked it, too, but it didn't make her feel any better. And, she had no intention of abandoning her new friends at the Golden Living retirement home. From the sound of it, Sylvia, and probably Marvin too, needed her help now more than ever. Something was going on that led to Forrest Spring's murder and she didn't think the police were looking down the right path.

Getting back into the rhythm of baking helped to calm her nerves. Measuring, mixing, pouring, and sliding trays into the oven felt therapeutic, and when the baking aromas filled the café, her mouth watered.

"Someone's hard at work," Mia said as she entered the café about twenty minutes after Tyler left. She poured herself some coffee, grabbed an apron, and sat at the counter. "When will Leona be back?"

"Sometime today, but I wanted to get ahead since I'll need to leave early today."

"Oh? Not something to do with what happened at Golden Living, I hope."

Annie felt her mother's eyes on her but kept her own on the muffin batter she poured into the pans. "I'm bringing Roxy over for a therapy visit. We went yesterday and they asked if we'd come back."

Mia chuckled. "Nice evasion, but I can see right through your answer. And Martha told me what you found in the bathroom yesterday."

Annie wiped her hands on her apron after she slid the pan in the oven. She leaned on the counter across from her mother. "Tyler was here this morning. He admitted that the gun I found is the murder weapon and it belonged to Sylvia. She needs my help now more than ever. If I visit with Roxy, it's an easy way to ask a few questions. People let their guard down when they have a dog to fuss over."

"I know I can't stop you, but please, Annie, be careful. Whoever is the murderer won't like you sticking your nose where it doesn't belong."

Annie finally met her mother's eyes. She nodded. "I'm always careful."

"And one more thing." Mia looked out the French doors before she continued. "Martha and Sylvia have been friends for a long time." She moved her eyes to meet Annie's. "That might cloud Martha's view of Sylvia. Be sure to keep an open mind."

"Are you saying that you think Sylvia shot Forrest?"

"No, I'm only saying, keep an open mind, which means that you need to consider that possibility. Don't forget, she was in Dawn's office, the murder weapon belongs to her, and there is something else you don't know about Sylvia."

"What," Annie laughed, "are you going to say she murdered someone in her past?"

Mia did not laugh or even crack a smile.

Goosebumps covered Annie's body.

"She killed her husband twenty years ago but it was ruled self-defense. She shot him."

Annie's hand shot up to cover her mouth. "You're kidding."

"I'm afraid not, Annie. Just be sure you look at the *whole* picture and not what you want to see."

CHAPTER 12

By the time Leona arrived at the Black Cat Café at the end of Friday morning, all giddy from her short vacation, Annie was chafing at the bit to leave.

"I've got good news and bad news," Annie told Leona. Her stomach was in knots with the thought of disappointing Leona by having to leave early.

"Me too. I'll go first. The good news is that this is going to be a busy, busy weekend." Leona said as she tied on a lime green apron with stalking cats. "And...the bad news is this is going to be a busy, busy weekend. I hope you're ready for a long day."

"I...uh...have to leave as early as possible." Annie stuttered out her reply. "But, I managed to get plenty of pastries made ahead of time so you shouldn't—"

"Stop right there! You need to leave?"

"Listen," Annie mustered all her internal strength. "Something came up that was out of my control and I need to leave after lunch. "You can manage without me for one afternoon." After all, Annie reminded herself, Leona left Annie with no advance notice, leaving a whole dinner to cater.

Leona scowled but remained silent.

Annie made sure to avoid Leona's glaring stares during the busy lunchtime rush. Instead, her mother's words about Sylvia shooting her husband twenty years ago ran in a loop through her brain. But, she couldn't see how it was possible for Sylvia to be the murderer Wednesday night. She would have had to have made two trips into Dawn's office, kill Forrest during the second trip, hide the gun in the toilet tank, then hide in the closet and send Martha the text asking for help. That was a lot to fall into place perfectly in a short window of time.

At one-thirty, before she left the Black Cat Café, Annie put a selection of muffins in a bag. The rush was over and Leona actually smiled at Annie as she left.

Annie found her note to Jason from this morning on the dining room table with his addition at the bottom. Another big problem with running the Black Cat Café was not seeing her husband before she left for work. At least he said he would take care of dinner. Since it was Friday, she could expect candles, flowers, romantic music, along with something tasty. A relaxing evening to look forward to, at least. But she had to get through the rest of the day first.

Roxy's nails clicked on the floor as she danced around Annie. "A walk before we visit your new friends?"

At the sound of the word *walk*, Roxy stood on her back legs and gently rested her front paws on Annie. Annie ruffled Roxy's ears. "Let's go."

The storm clouds still hovered overhead, but the rain had stopped. With her nose to the ground, Roxy followed all the new scents along the trail. A few people either jogged or walked briskly along the trail but Annie's mind stayed on the puzzling clues surrounding the murder.

On her return home, as she came abreast of Thelma Dodd's house, Roxy dashed up the trail to Thelma's kitchen door, like she did the day before.

"Okay, we have time for a short stop." Roxy gave her no choice in the matter of making a visit. "With luck, she won't need help with her crossword puzzle," Annie said.

Thelma saw Annie and waved from her screened-in porch. "Just let yourselves in," she called from above. "I'll wait right here for you."

Roxy, of course, rushed ahead of Annie as soon as the kitchen door cracked open. Her head rested on Thelma's knee by the time Annie entered the porch. Thelma offered Roxy a dog cookie and, like always, Roxy gently took the treat.

At the sight of Thelma with Roxy, Annie suddenly had an idea. "How do you feel about a little outing today, Thelma?"

"Well, that sounds wonderful. Where are you thinking of taking me?" Thelma's eyes sparkled.

Annie sat in the chair across from Thelma. "Roxy and I are going to visit Golden Living again this afternoon. Since you told me you know Sylvia and Sean, I thought you might like to come along." She lowered her voice as if she was telling a deep, dark secret. "And if you need any more encouragement, I'm bringing muffins."

"That sounds like a bribe if I ever heard one, but I never said a bribe wouldn't work on me." She grinned and held out her hand. "Help me up, please."

"I'll get my car and be back for you in a jiffy."

"Roxy can wait here with me and, Annie?"

Annie turned to look at Thelma.

"Don't forget the muffins."

"Don't worry about that." Annie headed home thinking that when Roxy walked into the retirement home with a basket of muffins hanging from her mouth, and Thelma leaning on Annie's arm, everyone would be putty in her hands.

It was only about five minutes before Annie returned for Thelma and Roxy, the muffins safely tucked next to the driver seat. Thelma used her walker to get to the kitchen door and then relied on Annie to help her down the one step out of the house to the walk and a half dozen more steps to her car. Roxy jumped in the back and made herself comfortable in the middle of the back seat where she had the best view between the two front seats.

"Do you want me to chat with Seany?" Thelma asked.

Annie took a quick look at Thelma. "Sure. You want to renew your old friendship?" Of course, Annie wanted Thelma to butter Sean up but she didn't want Thelma to think she was only using her to get information.

Thelma reached across the front seat and patted Annie's arm. "Don't worry. I don't mind picking his brain to see if he knows anything about the murder. That is your plan, isn't it?"

"Thelma Dodd, I can't believe that's what you think," Annie said as she tried not to burst out laughing. "Am I that transparent?"

"I know you, Annie. And I'm glad to help." She pulled her newspaper out of her coat pocket. "I brought my crossword puzzle. Maybe Seany can help me. It will be my ice breaker. A way to talk without really being too direct. Guess what the theme is today?"

"Easter?"

"Uh-huh. I think I'm going to have a good old time as long as you don't get in my way."

"Now that's just mean. How could I get in your way?"

"Oh, you know, you sit next to me like I'm some kind of helpless old person and then take over the conversation by finishing all my thoughts for me. If I remember anything about Seany, he can see right through someone's intentions. He grew up having to read people when he got shoved from one house to another."

"I won't interfere as long as you promise to tell me anything you learn." Annie turned into the parking lot of Golden Living.

"Don't worry about that."

After Annie parked right near the front entryway, she turned to Thelma. "There's one more thing you might be able to help me with."

"Okay."

"Don't say okay yet, you don't even know what I'm about to ask you."

"I trust you aren't planning to put me in a dangerous situation or ask me to whack someone with my walker."

Annie laughed. "Now that you mention it, I like the whacking idea," she began. "But, no, nothing like that. Would you mind talking to the manager about moving into Golden Living?"

Thelma's face fell and her eyes narrowed. "Is this some trick to get me out of my house? My son keeps telling me it's not safe for me to be living alone."

"No. No. No. Nothing like that." Annie held her hands up. "I'm trying to learn more about how people pay to live at this place. Sylvia said she's running out of money and I think there could be a connection between Forrest's death and some money skimming or some kind of scam."

Thelma's mouth fell open.

"We can skip that if you want. I don't want you to pretend you're thinking about moving if it makes you uncomfortable to talk about your finances."

"I'm not shocked about what you've asked me to do, I'm shocked about what you think is going on. Of *course* I'll talk to that manager. What's her name?"

"Dawn Cross."

"Oh, Annie, she's going to regret having *me* across the table from her. I might appear to be an old, feeble woman on the outside, but I spent forty years teaching and disciplining kids. I. Have. Not. Lost. My. Touch." Thelma opened the car door. "Get over here and help me out of this car. We need to get this show started."

The afternoon might be even more interesting than Annie originally hoped. This last minute addition of having Thelma tag along was bringing an exciting new dimension and opening up new possibilities with her no-nonsense approach toward information gathering.

"Oh," Annie stopped walking, "if you can, try to get Dawn to open the safe in her office. Before Forrest was murdered, Sylvia said she saw cash inside. When I got to the office not long after the murder, the cash was gone."

"Another twist. You think the murderer cleaned out the safe?" Thelma's cheeks were flushed pink with excitement.

"Maybe, or someone else did."

They started walking again. Thelma held onto her walker and Annie held Thelma's arm with one hand and Roxy's leash and the bag of muffins with her other hand. "It's been much too long since anything exciting happened in my life. This sure beats doing the crossword puzzle."

As soon as the door quietly closed behind them, Dawn appeared. She frowned when she saw Roxy in the lead but quickly replaced her displeasure with a smile when she saw Thelma.

"Hello, Annie," Dawn's syrupy-sweet voice said a bit too loudly. "Is this your friend you mentioned yesterday?"

"As a matter of fact, it is. Thelma Dodd, this is Dawn Cross, manager here at Golden Living."

"Come, come. Follow me. Thelma and I can chat in my office while you take your dog to the sunroom." Dawn waved her hand, gesturing them to hurry up.

"That sounds nice, but first I am planning to visit with a couple of my friends that live here," Thelma said.

Dawn stopped dead in her tracks. "Who would that be?"

"Sylvia May and Sean Woodman. Annie promised to bring her therapy dog back for a visit and I decided to tag along. I hope that's all right?" Thelma had a sweet expression on her face. Annie covered her mouth and pretended to cough to mask her choked laughter.

Dawn nodded. "Of course." Dawn also covered her mouth, but not before Annie caught the frown that replaced her fake smile.

Of course Dawn couldn't say no to a prospective customer, Annie thought. Her, *of course*, certainly wasn't an expression of happiness with Thelma's plan to visit with her friends.

"And Annie brought muffins for my friends," Thelma added. "From the Black Cat Café."

Dawn's eyes traveled to the bag and she swallowed. Annie had no intention of offering her a muffin.

"I'll bring Thelma to your office after our visit," Annie said as she tightened her grip on the muffin bag.

"What a lovely building," Thelma said. They walked down the hallway behind Dawn, her voice loud enough for anyone to hear. "I can't wait to find out how Sylvia and Sean like living here."

Dawn's shoulders tensed and Annie didn't miss the flinch. It was unlikely that Thelma would receive a glowing report from her two friends and Dawn just confirmed that she knew it. She would have her work cut out on her sales pitch when Thelma finally sat down in the manager's office.

CHAPTER 13

The sunroom was not as cozy on this dreary Friday afternoon as it was with all the sunshine streaming in the day before. But despite the change in weather, one thing remained exactly the same: Sean's wheelchair was parked in the same corner and his face held the same miserable glare.

Marvin was the first to spot Annie and he came right over. "What's in your bag?"

"Hello, Marvin. How about you bring Roxy around to visit everyone and then I'll share what's in my bag." She handed him the leash without waiting for a reply.

Sylvia was sitting with Martha but she looked up when Annie rested her hand on her shoulder. "I brought someone with me today."

Sylvia's forehead creased, then her eyes widened "Thelma? Thelma Dodd?"

"Hello Sylvia. Annie kindly invited me to come visit with her today. Can I join you?"

"Of course." Sylvia quickly rose and pulled up a chair for Thelma. "I suppose you heard about what happened this week?" she asked as she helped Thelma get comfortable.

"I certainly did." She looked at Sylvia and Martha. "My son thinks I shouldn't be living alone anymore and I thought Golden Living might be an option. But..."

Sylvia checked over her shoulder, leaned close to Thelma, and lowered her voice. "You *should* be concerned. When I moved in, I was assured that my money would last until I died, but now Dawn Cross says I have to move out at the end of the month." Her eyes filled with water but she blinked them away before any spilled out.

"Oh, dear. That's awful. What are you going to do?" Thelma asked, her voice full of concern for her old friend.

"I have no idea, but that's not even the worst of it. There's something else you probably don't know unless Annie told you; I'm a suspect in this terrible murder."

"Sylvia, that's the worst thing I've heard in ages. You were always the sweetest person in our group. Is it because of that, uh, problem with your husband?"

Sylvia twisted her hands in her lap. "I don't know. There's so much that keeps ending up on my plate—I was hiding in the office at the time of the murder, the murder weapon, my past—do you know what I think?"

Martha, Thelma, and Annie all leaned inches away from Sylvia.

"I think someone is framing me. Someone that wants me out of here."

"Dawn?" Martha asked.

Sylvia nodded. "She wants me out so she can get someone new in and steal *their* money." Her voice was strong and assured with that statement.

"So, if I move in," Thelma said, "I could be her next victim." She rubbed her hands together. "Dawn Cross won't know what's coming," she said with glee.

Sylvia frowned before the meaning of Thelma's words sank in. She leaned as close as possible and put her arm around Thelma's shoulders. "You always did have that rebel streak. I admired that quality and wished I could be more like you."

"Are you kidding? You're the one who let that no-good abusive husband know what end of your gun he didn't want to be looking at. That took more guts than anything I ever did."

"I was desperate. If I didn't shoot him, he would have killed me. But now it looks like he has come back to haunt me."

Annie took a quick peek around the room to make sure Marvin and Roxy were doing their job. Marvin was trying not to look bored but he stood tall and still, with a slight grin on his face, as Roxy enjoyed all the attention from various men and women.

Another resident caught her attention as he pushed himself toward Annie and her friends.

"Thelma Dodd? Is that you?"

The whole room became silent. Was it so unusual for Sean to leave his corner and talk to someone, Annie wondered.

Thelma turned her head as Sean Woodman approached. "Seany? It's been ages. How *are* you?"

Sean's eyes darted nervously to each pair of eyes staring at him. "Would you like to visit in my apartment?" He nodded his head toward the door out of the sunroom. "It's next door and I find it a bit too crowded in here for my taste."

Thelma pushed herself off the seat and Annie lined up her walker for her to follow Sean. She whispered in Thelma's ear, "Good luck bringing a smile to *his* face."

Marvin sat down in the seat vacated by Thelma and handed Roxy's leash to Annie. He eyed the bag in her lap.

"Should we go to your apartment, Sylvia?" Annie asked with a hushed voice. "I brought some muffins but I don't have enough for everyone in here."

Martha stood first. "Good idea. I can make tea while we do some brainstorming." She stared directly at Marvin. "It's high time you share some of your snooping details so we can get Sylvia out of this terrible predicament."

Marvin's mouth flopped open like a peeping chick begging for a morsel of food.

Annie moved the open bag under Marvin's nose. His mouth snapped shut and he followed Martha. Annie and Roxie stayed even with Sylvia as they left the sunroom.

"Do you think Thelma will get anywhere with her old friend?" Annie asked Sylvia.

"You mean Shady Sean? If anyone can get him to talk, it'll be Thelma. She has a way about her that you just can't ignore. The real question is whether what he tells her is true or not."

"I hadn't thought of that." Annie chuckled. "Maybe she can get him to put his guard down while he helps her with her crossword puzzle. Today she's planning to use it as the ice breaker with Sean."

Sylvia's forehead creased. "She had a plan to talk to Sean all along?"

"Yup, she's helping me do some digging around to see if we can find out what happened to your money and to Forrest."

Sylvia's eyes opened wide with fear. "You think Sean had something to do with all that?"

"Marvin told me that Forrest was about the only person Sean talked to, so I think he knows *something*."

"Now that you mention it, they *were* chummy." She stopped with her hand on her apartment door. "Forrest showed up a lot and visited with different people, especially Sean. I always thought he was being kind, but maybe he had another goal in mind."

Exactly what Annie was beginning to think; another goal which might have been connected to the missing money but ultimately got him murdered instead of making him rich.

Sylvia walked into her apartment ahead of Annie.

"It's about time you got here," Marvin said with his typical impatient tone. "What's in your bag?"

"Hold your Easter bunnies." Annie opened the bag and set it on Sylvia's small table. "It will be easier if I put everything on a plate."

Marvin tried to reach into the bag but Annie slapped his hand away. "Not so fast."

Marvin slumped into a chair and sulked like a two-year-old.

"So, Marvin, what can you tell us about Forrest and Sean?" Annie held the plate of muffins just out of reach as an obvious bribe.

"Wait a minute," Martha interrupted. "Sylvia, what happened to the Norman Rockwell lithograph you used to have hanging right here?" Martha pointed to a spot on Sylvia's wall that was brighter than the surrounding faded blue.

Martha flicked her hand dismissively. "That old thing? I didn't like it anymore."

"Sylvia? That hung in your parents' living room. Your mother loved it. If you don't want it, I'll hang it in *my* house." Martha stared at her friend but Sylvia's eyes roamed around her apartment, looking at everything except Martha.

In a very small voice, she finally responded, "I sold it."

Martha's eyes softened with moisture. She hugged Sylvia. "You should have told me. I would have helped. Who did you sell it to? Maybe we can buy it back."

"That was my plan, but I'm afraid it's gone forever." She sagged onto her chair. "Forrest found a buyer for me so we can't ask him now, can we?"

Marvin finished his blueberry muffin and helped himself to another while everyone was distracted with Sylvia's problem. "I know where it is," he said in between bites.

Sylvia, Martha, and Annie stared at him.

"Finally, you can make yourself useful," Annie said as she offered muffins to the others before Marvin ate everything.

"Sean bought it," Marvin stated. He carefully wiped each finger with his crisp white handkerchief before refolding it and sliding it in his pants pocket. "I overheard them whispering in the sunroom last week. Sean kept telling Forrest to be quiet but Forrest just kept yammering on and on. It was quite obvious that he didn't like the terms Sean offered him for the deal."

Annie sat next to Marvin. "What else do you know about Sean?" She set the remaining muffins near him and twisted her body so she faced him directly.

"I saw him go into Dawn's office the night before Forrest was murdered."

"Did you see what he did in there?"

"No, but he had a folder in his lap when he went in. I heard some papers being shuffled around.

Annie sat back in her chair. "We have to find out what's in Dawn's folders. I saw a stack of them in the open safe before I found Sylvia in the closet. Marvin, I suspect you know this building better than anyone. Is there some way we can get a look at those folders?"

"Maybe. Dawn always opens the safe to add new paperwork before she leaves for the day. If someone creates a distraction, she might forget to close it before she goes to investigate. Of course, she'll return at some point but you might be able to sneak in and take a look while she's out of the office. It's a long shot."

Martha offered a more drastic plan. "We could just knock her over the head after she opens it. Take the folders and leave."

"As appealing as that sounds," Annie said, "I have a better idea. I'll discuss it with Thelma since she'll have to be okay with her part."

"Thelma will love whatever you have planned," Sylvia said. "She always did the opposite of what our parents expected. She loved a bit of drama and excitement and I doubt she's changed. As a matter of fact, she can always use the age card to excuse her behavior if necessary."

Marvin stood. "Can I take the rest of the muffins?"

Annie shoved the two leftover muffins in the bag. "I'd love to give them to you, but I need something to offer Thelma and Sean. I'll make you more, what's your favorite?"

His face lit up. "My mother used to make cream cheese brownie cupcakes and I haven't had one in years. Could you make that for me?"

Annie smiled. She'd do anything to keep Marvin on her side, and if it meant plying him with baked goods, well, that was a small price to pay.

"I think I can manage that."

"One more thing," Marvin said before Annie got to the door. "Don't forget to distract Gloria, too. She likes to poke her nose in Dawn's business whenever possible. Those two are like two rival teenagers after the same boy. Only, the prize around here isn't a boy, it's having control of this place."

"Great. I'll see if I can pull Thelma away from Shady Sean and get going with some undercover shenanigans."

"His apartment is the last door on the left. Right next to the sunroom."

Annie and Roxy headed down the hall toward Sean's apartment. "Come on Roxy, let's see if this guy warms up to you and an apple raisin muffin as easily as Marvin did."

CHAPTER 14

Annie knocked on the door of Sean Woodman's apartment. She hoped that Thelma had managed to warm him up in the last hour. His steely glare when she saw him in the sunroom was enough to curdle milk.

The door opened into a spacious, sunny apartment. "You're Thelma's friend?"

"Yes." Annie held out her hand. "Annie Hunter, and this is Roxy. Could we come in for a minute?" She glanced past Sean. The first thing that caught her attention was a Norman Rockwell lithograph.

Sean didn't bother to shake Annie's hand or pat Roxy who stood quietly next to her. "Thelma and I are about finished talking."

Annie took a step through the door. "I have muffins from the Black Cat Café if you'd like one." She smiled.

"Seany, invite Annie in. She doesn't bite." Thelma's voice came from around the corner. "It's about time you try to be a bit more sociable."

Sean sighed and rolled his wheelchair into the living room. Thelma sat in front of a large window that overlooked a courtyard filled with ornamental shrubs bursting with buds. Birds chirped and landed on the various feeders; a welcome contrast to the chill in the apartment.

"Isn't this lovely? Seany has the best apartment in the whole building. The sunroom shares that wall and offices are on the other two walls. It's really two apartments converted into one."

Annie looked out the window at the courtyard. The square enclosed space had a stone walkway that led from Sean's door to a gate on the far side of the sunroom wall. It would be possible for someone to get to his apartment without going through the front entrance. Or, likewise, he could leave unnoticed.

Roxy took up her usual spot when she visited Thelma, placing her head on Thelma's knee. "I don't have my dog bones here, Roxy. Sorry about that." She stroke Roxy's head and fiddled with her silky ears.

Annie held her bag with two muffins toward Thelma. She happily helped herself. "I've been thinking about this the whole time I've been here. Try one, Seany. Annie is a fantastic baker."

Thelma pointed to the chair near her. "Make yourself comfortable. I'm not ready to visit with Dawn yet."

Sean's eyebrows shot up. "What are you visiting with her for?"

"Oh, didn't I tell you? I'm thinking about moving in. Well, it's my son, really. He doesn't think I should live alone anymore." She tasted her muffin. "Delicious.

Take one, Seany. You need to put a little meat on those bones of yours before you disappear."

Annie didn't think Sean was used to anyone telling him what to do, or, at least, not following those instructions *if* someone had the nerve to tell him what to do. She also noticed him flinch a bit when Thelma called him Seany.

He took the last muffin.

Thelma babbled along. "Seany told me he knew that poor boy who was murdered, right Seany?"

"I saw him around a few times."

"Don't by bashful, you said he even came in to visit you here, play a little chess now and then."

Sean kept his face neutral as Thelma carried the conversation and he sized up Annie.

"Do you think Thelma would like living here?" Annie asked Sean. She decided he certainly wasn't going to offer anything, so why not just ask away.

"She seems to be enjoying herself today, but visiting and living here are two different things, I suppose." He had finally managed to finish the muffin without making a mess in his lap.

"I'm a little concerned," Thelma said. "Especially after Sylvia told me her money ran out and she has to leave at the end of the month. Can you believe it?"

"Sylvia? The woman you were sitting with in the sunroom?"

"Yes, that's the one. She doesn't know what she's going to do."

"She's the one that was in Dawn's office when Forrest was murdered? Maybe she won't have to worry if she ends up in a jail cell."

"Seany! Don't talk like that. Sylvia is no more a murderer than you are. Who might want that poor boy dead?"

Sean shrugged. "I try to stay out of everyone's business. Much easier that way." He checked his watch.

"Should we head to the office, Thelma?" Annie asked. Even if Thelma didn't pick up on Sean's readiness for them to leave, she did, and she didn't want to overstay a barely lukewarm visit.

"I suppose so. Or maybe we should just head home and come back another day. This outing has been more for me than I'm used to, I'm afraid. In case you haven't noticed, I'm not as young as I used to be." She chuckled. "And I'm tired."

"Whatever you want. I'm sure Roxy would love to visit again tomorrow." Annie helped Thelma to her walker which rested next to a desk with several folders arranged neatly on one side. Annie's fingers itched to slip them in her bag but she could feel Sean's eyes boring into her back. She would need Thelma to make a diversion.

As if Thelma read Annie's mind, she suddenly remembered something to ask Sean. "I almost forgot. You said you'd let me borrow your photo album from when we were kids. Would it be too much trouble to get it for me?"

Annie saw his jaw clench but he humored Thelma. "It's in my bedroom, I'll be right back."

As soon as he was out of the room, Annie flipped the top folder open. She looked at Thelma who nodded and she quickly slipped the top paper out, folded it, and slid it into her pocket.

With the carpets muffling sound in Sean's apartment, she was surprised to see him behind her when she turned around. Her body was between the desk and his bedroom so she hoped he wouldn't have been able to see what she did.

"Here you go, Thelma. Keep it as long as you like." He handed the album to Thelma but she couldn't carry it while using her walker, so Annie reached over for it. Her hand brushed against the folder and sent it sliding across the desk, onto the floor with all the papers scattering everywhere.

"You clumsy woman!" Sean yelled.

"Really Seany, it was an accident," Thelma scolded.

Annie quickly scooped up the loose papers and shoved them back into the folder. "I'm so sorry for my clumsiness," Annie gushed. She picked up the photo album and held Thelma's elbow as they left Sean's apartment. She didn't know if it was only her imagination but it felt like Sean's eyes were burning a hole in her back.

"I never knew you to be so clumsy," Thelma said and giggled. "That was a brilliant move to mess up his papers."

"I hope it takes him a while to figure out which piece of paper is missing. If he figures it out at all."

"That whole visit was illuminating," Thelma said. "Seany is *not* the person I remember. He's angry, self-centered, and rude."

Annie looked at Thelma from the corner of her eyes. "And I thought the two of you were getting along thick as a warren of rabbits when I arrived. You won't be visiting anymore?"

"I'll be back. He hasn't seen the end of me. You wouldn't believe all the questions he asked about my house, my retirement, and how was I managing on my own. Other than that, I don't even think he listened to anything I had to say."

"How about the crossword puzzle?"

"That was a waste of time. I'm not sure what he does all day by himself in that apartment except sit at his computer. He said he doesn't eat in the dining hall or visit with any other residents. He has turned into a bitter old man."

"Pssst. Over here."

Annie peered into the shadow of a doorway and saw Marvin gesturing. "Follow me."

Annie, Roxy, and Thelma followed Marvin into his apartment. He closed the door. "What's the plan for a diversion? Dawn always opens her safe at four which only leaves us about ten minutes to get something started."

"Thelma's too tired, we'll have to do it tomorrow," Annie said.

"Tomorrow's Saturday. She doesn't open the safe on Saturday. It has to be now."

Thelma grinned. "I'm fine. I gave that line to Seany so he wouldn't get too suspicious about my activities. Fill me in on this plan about looking in a safe."

"We didn't exactly come up with a plan, but the first step is getting you into Dawn's office."

Marvin danced from one foot to the other. "Martha, Sylvia, and I made a plan. As soon as Dawn opens the safe, let go of Roxy. Sylvia will fake a fall and scream. I'll have some tasty dog treats and you send Roxy to help Sylvia. Dawn will have to investigate, it will be chaos and it should give you a few minutes to check the safe."

"As long as she doesn't slam it closed." Annie pointed out the biggest problem with the plan.

"Right. Timing is everything. You walk in right after she opens the safe to distract her." Marvin looked at Thelma. "Could you pretend to be dizzy or something so Dawn has to help you to a chair?"

"High school drama was a high point in my teenage years. I think I can remember a few skills."

"Are you up to this, Thelma? I don't want you to overdo it and really end up fainting," Annie said.

"This is the most excitement I've had for years. And if it helps Sylvia, I'll do anything."

Marvin checked the time. "You'd better get going. But remember, wait until she opens the safe before you go in."

"I think it's best if I leave Roxy with you now instead of relying on her to do her part. If you want her to start barking after Sylvia falls, show her a treat and tell her 'speak'."

Marvin happily took Roxy's leash. He crouched next to her and put his arm around her body. Annie was pretty sure he was whispering in her ear, too. The way to Marvin's heart was with a dog and a muffin, she told herself. But maybe in the reverse order.

As Annie and Thelma made their way toward the office, Thelma asked, "What was on that paper you took from Seany's folder?"

"I'm not sure. There was a list of names and numbers. It might be nothing, but by his reaction, I think there is something he isn't keen on sharing. And I noticed him flinch when you called him *Seany*. I don't think he likes it." They were almost even with Gloria's office door.

"I know. That's why I keep it up." She chuckled. "There's something about him that rubs me the wrong way but he hasn't got the nerve to be rude to me yet. My read is that as long as he thinks I have some value to him, he'll bite his tongue and play his version of nice."

Gloria's door opened. "I was hoping to catch you before you leave. I thought we could have a little chat about Golden Living." She held her arm out in a gesture for Annie and Thelma to enter.

"Um, Dawn is expecting me," Thelma said.

The smile on Gloria's face remained pasted on but a twitch in her eye indicated displeasure. "Annie, could I talk to you for a minute at least? You can catch up to your friend in no time."

Was this a plan to separate them so there was no witness to Dawn's conversation with Thelma? Or was it a power play on Gloria's part to undercut Dawn?

Annie suspected the latter. She had complete confidence in Thelma's ability to stand up to Dawn on her own. "Sure, no problem, Gloria. Go ahead Thelma, I'll join you in a jiffy."

Annie heard a clock start to chime just as Thelma reached Dawn's door. She crossed her fingers that the plan would work and followed Gloria into her office.

CHAPTER 15

Gloria turned on Annie. "You double crossed me," she hissed.

Annie jerked backwards as if the words actually hit her in the face.

"You talked to me first about your friend and then I find out you're all cozy with Dawn instead."

Okay, what the heck was going on at this place? If management didn't work together and get along, it certainly didn't bode well for anyone living at Golden Living.

Gloria sneered. "Don't let Dawn's friendly smile and suck up attitude fool you. All she cares about is getting her hands on your friend's money."

"Really? And I thought this was such a well-run establishment." Annie hoped Gloria didn't pick up on her sarcasm. "Are you telling me that my friend should steer clear of Golden Living?"

Gloria's tone softened. "No, sorry, not at all. I get pretty riled up about what's happening around here lately. It's just, well, Dawn is up to something but I'm keeping my eye on her."

Annie heard footsteps tapping on the tiles in the hallway. She steadied herself for the beginning of what she hoped would be a successful distraction, missing the rest of Gloria's conversation.

A crash.

"Help!" Sylvia's voice echoed outside Gloria's office door. "Help me!"

The sound of Roxy's nails clicking and footsteps rushing in the hall made Gloria stop talking and look past Annie.

The footsteps stopped. Roxy barked. "Are you alright?" Marvin's panicked voice boomed over everything else.

"What the heck?" Gloria said as she rushed into the hallway.

Annie took the opportunity to go through the open door that linked Gloria and Dawn's offices. Thelma sat like a limp sack of potatoes in one of the chairs with no one else in sight. Annie rushed to her side and knelt in front of her.

"Thelma? Are you okay?" Annie knew what the plan was but this was too real.

Thelma opened her eyes and winked at Annie. She whispered, "The safe."

The space was too far between Thelma and the open safe but something else caught Annie's attention. An open folder showing papers similar to what she took from Sean's apartment practically jumped into her hand.

Annie scooped up a few of the papers and shoved them into her pocket with the paper from Sean's apartment. "We've got to get out of here. If anyone asks, I'll say I'm taking you to the ER to get checked."

Thelma leaned heavily on Annie and her walker once they were in the hall. Sylvia sat on the floor surrounded by Martha, Dawn, Gloria, and some other people wearing Golden Living shirts.

Marvin, with Roxy, made his way to Annie's side and whispered, "All set?"

Annie nodded. "Help me get Thelma to my car. I have to get out of here."

Just as the trio reached the door, Dawn's voice stopped Annie dead in her tracks. "Annie. Wait a minute."

"Get Thelma and Roxy in my car. I'll take care of Dawn." Marvin continued on like he did this every day.

Annie walked back to meet Dawn who was rushing toward her. "Mrs. Dodd and I weren't done with our chat," she blurted out in a rush of words.

"She isn't feeling well and I need to get her to the doctor. Too much excitement I think."

"I hope she's okay. Be sure to bring her back. I think she'll love living here and I have an apartment opening up very soon. It won't be empty for long."

I'm not so sure about that, Annie thought. It's more likely that the whole place will be empty with all the possible scandals on the horizon. "Of course. I'll have her back for another visit as soon as she's up to it."

Annie turned away from Dawn, acting as casual as possible. When her hand touched the outside door, she couldn't help but take a quick glance back at the scene. Dawn stood staring at her. She raised her hand. "I have another question."

Before Dawn could move closer to Annie, Gloria pulled on Dawn's arm and pointed to Sylvia. With that distraction, Annie slipped out the door and hustled to her car. She sighed with relief to be safely away with the papers hidden in her pocket.

Thelma was sipping on some bottled water she must have brought in her bag and Marvin sat comfortably in the back seat with one arm draped over Roxy. "The coast is clear, you can get out now, Marvin," Annie said after she slid behind the wheel.

"Do I have to? I'd rather stay with you two."

Annie didn't expect that comment from grouchy Marvin. She turned around to look at him. "Listen. You need to stay here and keep Sylvia company. We can't all abandon her after her fantastic diversion. I'll tell

Martha to bring you and Sylvia to the Black Cat Café for breakfast tomorrow. Okay?"

Marvin let out a long sad sigh. "Okay. Maybe you could come back tonight instead?" The hopefulness was unmistakable.

"Maybe. Let me get out of here before Dawn figures out something is missing from one of her folders. If you disappear, she might suspect you with all your snooping activities. You need to be our ears here."

Marvin looked a tiny bit satisfied with the compliment. He got out and headed back into Golden Living. "We need to get both Marvin and Sylvia out of this place before someone else is killed," Annie said.

Thelma's eyes opened wide. "Do you think they're in danger? They could stay with me for a few days. I have that whole big house all to myself. I know my son wouldn't be happy, but too bad. And you live only a few houses away if we needed any help."

"That's very generous." Yes, it was generous, but Annie wasn't sure it was a *good* idea. Especially since they would be her responsibility. Oh dear, what did she get herself in the middle of? A murder, stolen information, and now three elderly people looking to her for help. What was Jason going to say if she showed up for their romantic dinner with two old ladies and a grumpy old man with her?

"Annie, did you hear me?" Thelma said.

"Sorry, I guess I was daydreaming."

"I've made up my mind. I think you should go back to pick up Sylvia and Marvin. They can stay with me until all this drama settles down. I don't want it on my conscience if something happens to one or both of them that I didn't do everything I could to help."

"How about I call Martha? She's there with Sylvia and she can bring them over. I'm sure they can cook up some excuse why they're leaving if anyone asks."

"Perfect." Thelma fidgeted in her seat. "I don't have enough food to feed everyone."

And before Annie's brain processed what her mouth was about to do, words fell right out. "You can all eat at my house tonight."

Thelma clapped her hands. "I knew you'd help. You're always so generous."

If only Thelma knew what Annie was *really* thinking. She might not come to the conclusion that Annie was so generous after all. She just had a problem saying no.

Once Annie arrived home, she made sure Thelma was settled comfortably on her porch before she called Martha and shared the latest plan. Martha said they would leave soon which left one more call for Annie to make.

"Jason? You know that nice dinner you planned for the two of us tonight?"

"I'll be home shortly. Can't wait." His cheerful voice made her feel good but she knew her next words would disappoint him.

"Can you bring enough for at least four more people? Well, better make it six more." Annie decided to let her mother and Leona know what was going on and get their help, too.

Jason didn't respond.

"Are you still there?" Annie asked.

"Uh, I am. Do I even want to know what's going on?"

"Probably not." She laughed. "But I'll tell you anyway. I brought Thelma Dodd to visit some friends at Golden Living today and they're all coming to our house tonight. Is that okay?"

"Are they sleeping at our house, too?"

"No. They'll stay with Thelma, but she didn't have enough food for them."

"I'm confused, but you can fill me in when I get home. I'll pick up pizza. How does that sound?"

"I have no idea, but it will have to do for a last minute plan, right? I'll let them know that no complaints are allowed."

Jason laughed. "Good luck with that, and I don't even know who's coming besides Thelma."

Right. Marvin would most likely complain about something but she was used to him now. "Don't worry. You'll like everyone. And, Jason?"

"There's more?"

"I have some papers I need you to help me go over to see if there's something unusual happening at Golden Living."

"Don't tell me any more details. I'd rather not know how you got the papers. Listen, I just pulled into the pizza place so try not to round up any more people before I'm home in, let's see, forty-seven-and-a-half minutes. Bye."

At least he still had his sense of humor. "Bye." Annie hoped no one else showed up too, because the only people she could think of that *might* drop in were the exact people she did *not* want to see—Detective Crank, Police Chief Johnson, or anyone from Golden Living.

She figured she had some time before Martha arrived with their guests. She called her mother and Leona and without giving any details invited them over for pizza. Leona sounded like she was completely over the fact that Annie left work early and thought it was a great idea. She even offered to bring dessert. Annie could tell that her mother sensed something was up but she didn't ask for any details and offered to bring some wine. Wine wasn't the perfect match with pizza but it certainly would help mellow her nerves.

Annie fixed a tray with crackers, cheese, veggies, and dip and brought it to the porch. She smiled at the sight of Thelma with two cats curled up on her lap and Roxy at her side like always. "You're the animal whisperer, Thelma."

"This is the best day I've had in so long. I'm not complaining about my life, mind you, and I love my porch and my routine, but today sure did shake up my adrenaline. In a good way."

Annie held the tray so Thelma could help herself to a few snacks. "You were amazing today. If those papers reveal a scam, it's all thanks to your acting." And if they didn't, Annie didn't even want to consider where they would search next or what it might mean for Sylvia.

"I can't stop thinking about Seany. I know life handed him a basket of trouble, but that's no excuse if he's involved with scamming those seniors out of their money. Have you looked at any of those papers yet?"

Annie sat on a wicker rocking chair. "Not yet. I'm going to have Jason help me after dinner." Annie helped herself to a slice of cheese and a cracker and enjoyed the view of the lake. "We're pretty lucky to have a spot on the edge of Heron Lake."

Thelma nodded in agreement. "Seany got pretty excited when I told him where I lived. I swear I saw dollar signs pop up in his eyeballs along with a ka-ching. How will he be stopped? People like Sylvia shouldn't be cheated and thrown out on the street. How do you think he does it?"

"Hold on a minute. We don't know what, if anything, Sean is actually doing. And even if he has some incriminating information on people who live at Golden Living, it doesn't mean he has stolen from anyone. Right now, the most important thing is to find out how Forrest was connected to any of this to get himself murdered."

"I forgot about that," Thelma said. "Maybe he discovered what was going on and threatened to go to the police."

"Or maybe he was part of the scam and wanted a bigger cut."

"Oh dear. I'm not very good at seeing all the possibilities."

Annie stood. "That's why we all need to talk about what's happening and see what we can put together. You know Sean the best; Sylvia was friendly with Forrest; and Marvin probably has the most information about Golden Living from all his snooping. We'll have to convince him to share what he knows. But if I ply him with sweets and Roxy gives him her best sad eyes, he'll be like bread dough in my hands."

"Ah," Thelma said knowingly. "The way to Marvin's heart—food and a dog!"

CHAPTER 16

Leona was the first to barge through the door into Annie's house, carrying a big box from the Black Cat Cafe. "Mia gave me a quick summary of what I missed. How do you manage to get pulled into so much drama in the blink of an eye?"

"I also managed to pull off the best dinner that the residents at Golden Living ever had," Annie said with her eyebrows raised. "You are welcome for that, Leona."

"Oh, right, thanks. But a murder? Right under your nose? Why can't you walk away and let the police deal with everything instead of trying to save everyone?"

"Shhh!" Annie put her finger to her lips and nodded toward the porch. "I have guests for dinner, did you forget?"

Leona poked her head through the door to see who was on the porch. "Oh, hello Thelma."

"Let me tell you something, Leona Robinson. You could take some lessons from Annie about what's important. She knows the value of her family and friends. Instead of saying 'no, I can't,' she always says 'yes.' Even if it's inconvenient." Thelma raised one eyebrow like she was scolding a little girl in one of her classrooms from long ago. As a matter of fact, maybe

Leona had been the recipient of exactly one of those scoldings. "Do you understand me?"

"Yes, Mrs. Dodd."

Annie snickered behind her hand at Leona's chastised expression. When Thelma put it like that, she felt guilty for her earlier thoughts about resenting this invasion on her romantic dinner. She and Jason could postpone their dinner for two, but time wasn't making a detour with Sylvia's future on the line.

Martha opened the door and ushered Sylvia and Marvin inside.

"Wow. Can I move in here?" Marvin asked as he looked around the spacious and cozy downstairs of Annie and Jason's house. "I'd even be willing to pay for a room."

"Be quiet, Marvin," Sylvia scolded. "Annie isn't running a retirement home. Just be thankful for a night out."

Annie rolled her eyes. "Thelma's on the porch. Make yourselves comfortable while we wait for dinner to arrive."

"What are you feeding us?" Marvin asked. "I can't eat seafood, just so you know. And too much of those black bean dishes and no one's gonna want to be in the same room with me."

"Marvin!" Sylvia hissed. "I told you to turn on your best behavior. No one wants to hear about your digestive issues. Now go sit down and try to find something nice to say."

Leona and Annie exchanged a glance. "Interesting dinner guests," Leona said. The corners of her lips twitched with amusement. "I can't wait until Jason arrives to your dinner party."

Annie was thinking along those same lines. But Jason would rally and he might even take a liking to Marvin's brand of say-it-like-it-is. "Leona, how was your vacation?"

Leona closed her eyes and sighed a deep moan of satisfaction. "Better than I imagined. Danny booked us a suite in an elegant bed and breakfast with a view of the ocean. With the windows cracked, the sound of waves crashing on the beach, and the ocean breeze blowing the gauzy curtains, I felt like a princess in a fairytale."

Maybe a couple of peas to annoy her sleep? Annie was happy for Leona but at the same time, she felt a pinch of jealousy at the thought of Leona lounging while Annie ran around like a rabbit trying to avoid becoming a fox's dinner. An uncomfortable mattress would be a small consolation prize. "Did you find any peas under the mattress?"

"Nope. The mattress was the comfiest I've ever slept in. The food wasn't great, though. But I washed dinner down with plenty of wine so it didn't matter in the end. Speaking of wine, Mia said she was bringing some. Where is she? This crowd might be even more interesting after a couple of glasses of vino." She grinned.

The outside door opened, filling the kitchen with a delicious, stomach-growling aroma of pizza crust, hot cheese, and zesty spices. Mia held the door for Jason and his armful of pizza boxes.

Leona relieved Mia of her wine bag. "Finally. You two are in for a treat. I'll get glasses for the wine; we'll all need it."

Jason looked around the kitchen-dining-living space. "Where did you hide your guests, Annie?" A burst of laughter erupted from the porch. "Ahhh. A quick summary of what's going on?"

Leona handed full wine glasses around.

"You all know Thelma Dodd who lives a few houses away?"

Leona, Jason, and Mia nodded.

"She came with me and Roxy to Golden Living for a visit. Coincidentally, she has a couple of acquaintances who live there—Sylvia and a guy named Sean, who might be involved with a scam that's draining people like Sylvia of their money and forcing them to move."

"That's terrible. Did you uncover more details?" Mia asked. "Wasn't Sylvia the one in the closet when Forrest was murdered?"

"Yes. And I suspect this whole money-murder thing is connected."

"To this Sean guy?" Jason wondered.

"Well, he could be involved, but there's also the manager, Dawn, and her secretary, Gloria, who are in some kind of power struggle. The bottom line is that someone murdered Forrest Spring while he was in Dawn's office and the safe was open and all the money disappeared. I find it hard to believe that the open safe, the missing money, and the murder were only coincidences."

Leona tilted her head toward the porch. "So why the meeting of the seniors?"

"A complication, sort of."

Jason relaxed in his recliner. "I'm guessing you're finally getting to the part of the story that has something to do with how you ended up with the papers you mentioned to me on the phone?"

Annie put plates and napkins on the table. "Thelma, along with Sylvia and Roxy, created a diversion when Dawn's safe was open and somehow a few of the papers on Dawn's desk ended up in my pocket. Thelma didn't want to abandon Sylvia when Dawn made the discovery and Marvin kind of added himself to the mix."

"Ended up in your pocket? I wonder how that happened. Did they grow legs?" Leona snorted. "You do have a knack for jumping from one little pile of rotten eggs into a whole basket of them."

"Are you waiting for that food to get cold before you invite us in?" Marvin's silent entry and interruption made Annie jump. "You know, we aren't getting any younger out here. Me and Sylvia are accustomed to eating at exactly four-thirty. And it's well past six." Marvin stood in the doorway with his hands on his hips. "Well?"

"It's Sylvia and I," Thelma corrected as she pushed her walker past Marvin. "And you can get at the end of the line."

Marvin's mouth flopped open. He obviously wasn't used to anyone bossing him around but he did let Thelma, Sylvia, and Martha get their pizza before he dared take a plate.

With his pizza on his plate and a drink in his hand, Marvin started to follow Martha to the porch but stopped. "Could I sit in here at the table instead?"

"You'd rather take your chances with the younger crowd?" Leona teased.

"Those three keep ganging up on me."

Jason slapped Marvin on the back. "You and I need to stick together against all these females. Have a seat and I'll be right over to join you after I help myself to some of the pizza."

Annie shoved a bottle of wine in Leona's hand. "How about you and Mia entertain the ladies on the porch?" She tilted her head slightly toward Marvin and raised her eyebrows.

Mia, always quicker on the uptake than her sister, grabbed Leona's arm. "Come on. It's a beautiful evening to sit outside with our dinner."

Perfect, Annie thought. Now, with Jason as her helper, maybe together they'd be able to pull information out of Marvin. Annie sat across from him. "I see you took the meat lovers pizza."

Marvin was already half done with one piece. "None of that girly, no meat stuff for me. All those vegetables—"

"How long have you lived at Golden Living?" Annie interrupted before Marvin went into a description of his intestinal issues. She had already heard more than enough of that sort of information from him.

"*Too* long is how long."

Annie felt Jason kick her under the table as he took over the conversation. "Tell me, Marvin, do you have any kids?"

"Two no-good sons who sold my house so I'm stuck living where I am. I worked for forty years and now I've got nothing to show for it." He started on his second piece of pizza.

"What kind of work did you do?"

Marvin stopped chewing and turned his head toward Jason. "Why? What difference does it make?"

Jason leaned back in his chair. "Here's the thing. You strike me as a hard worker. Someone who keeps his eye on what's going on. Am I right?"

Marvin nodded and puffed up his chest a little with the compliment.

"Sometimes I need an extra hand around here. You know, keep an eye on our house and the animals if we go away for the weekend or something like that." Jason winked at Annie.

"Would you feed me, too?"

"Of course. I'm always looking for the right guy for that responsibility. Would you be interested?"

Marvin sat up straighter and puffed his chest out even more. "You bet I am. I keep an eye on the comings and goings at Golden Living. Not that anyone knows, but it's what I do."

"About that—" Annie began, but Jason kicked her again.

"What Annie wonders is, how did you develop that talent?" Annie smiled. Jason definitely phrased that question better than she would have.

Marvin set the crust of his pizza on the edge of his plate and looked toward the porch. In a hushed voice he said, "It's not something I talk about."

Jason put his hand on Marvin's forearm. Annie expected to see him flinch and pull away but, instead, he looked at Jason and said, "You have a lot of compassion. Not like so many others."

Annie's heart cracked when she heard the sadness in Marvin's voice. What happened to him to cause such despair?

"What others, Marvin?" Jason asked with a gentleness in his voice.

Marvin's eyes filled but he pulled himself together before even one drop leaked out. His eyes hardened.

Annie held her breath, waiting for Marvin to continue.

"When I was a working man, I let my guard down one day and thugs robbed the office." He shrugged. "I can remember every detail like it happened yesterday. Their guns, their masks, their angry voices, and the whack on my head that left a scar." His fingers absentmindedly rubbed a spot on the back of his head.

"It wasn't your fault." Annie was horrified and she wanted to console Marvin.

He blinked and looked at her. "It was my job to keep everyone safe. I failed but it won't happen again if I can help it."

"But what about Forrest?" Annie regretted her question as soon as it left her mouth.

Marvin's face tensed. "He wasn't my responsibility. He made his own problems by cozying up to the wrong people. I watch out for the people *living* at Golden Living, and," he leaned close to Jason and Annie, "something's not right."

That was an understatement. Annie couldn't keep the thought from niggling in the back of her mind that maybe Marvin killed Forrest, thinking he was protecting everyone at Golden Living.

Was she looking into the eyes of a cold-blooded murderer?

The thought saddened her, and at the same time, it gave her chills.

CHAPTER 17

Annie was exhausted when she closed the door behind the last of her dinner guests, but her work for the night wasn't over. She pulled out the papers that she'd taken from Golden Living and sat at the dining room table with Jason and another glass of wine.

Jason put his hand on top of the papers. "You know, we could just turn these over to the police and let them see where it leads."

"We could." Annie pushed Jason's hand off. "But I'm not going to. If we find something, then we can make a plan."

Jason gently pushed Annie's hand away, effectively covering the papers again. "How will you explain how this information landed on *our* table?"

Annie sipped her wine. "If what I think, and Marvin also seems to believe, indicates something illegal is going on related to how Golden Living gets money from the residents, whoever misses these papers won't be going to the police."

"Good point. They'll be going after you. Did you think of that?"

"I wasn't even in Dawn's office, as far as she knows. Thelma fainted, Sylvia fell in the hallway, there was such confusion and with so many people around, any one of them could have taken the papers. With a few hints strategically dropped and the rumor mill spreading them, it might just play into the power struggle between Dawn and Gloria."

Jason stroked his chin. "Tell me more about those two. Dawn is the manager and Gloria is the secretary?"

"Right. Dawn switches between super nice and super rude; Gloria probably runs the show, at least behind the scenes, and I think she wants more credit and possibly more money. Martha heard through the Golden Living grapevine that she might have an addiction to prescription drugs which would put her in the market for some easy cash."

"If that's true."

"Of course, if it's true."

With his hand still on the pile of papers, Jason asked, "What are you hoping to find in here?"

"I'm not sure. Sylvia said her money is running out and she has to move at the end of the month, but when she moved in, she got assurances that there was plenty of money for her to stay as long as she needed to. Where did her money disappear to?"

Jason considered this information. "You need to get her bank statements and any other financial information so we can compare that to what may be in here. We can look for transfers to mysterious accounts for starters, but it won't be easy. Does she have anyone, maybe a close family member, looking out for her?"

"No. She's on her own. Well, except for Martha who visits a lot, but I don't think she's been helping Sylvia with her finances."

Jason's face lit up. "You may be on to something, Annie. We need to make a list of people at Golden Living who are on their own; no family or a close friend to keep an eye on their finances. They would be an easier target for anyone who is savvy about digging on the computer. It could be anyone at Golden Living targeting and taking advantage of those who are vulnerable."

"You mean, have them sign everything over and *trust* that Golden Living would take care of them? Who would be that naïve?"

"It's probably more complicated than that, but it makes sense to consider people on their own as the most plausible place to start to look for some type of money shenanigans."

Annie took one last paper from her pocket. "And there's this." She unfolded the paper and placed it on top of the rest.

Jason's eyes traveled between the paper and Annie. "What is it and how does it fit in with the other information?"

Annie shifted in her chair and idly stroked Smokey who purred contentedly in her lap. "Thelma visited with someone at Golden Living who she used to know, Sean Woodman. He doesn't interact with the other people living there but he did invite Thelma into his apartment. When I picked her up to go home, it was spacious, nice big windows facing a courtyard with an outside access. Thelma said it's two apartments converted into one."

"It sounds like he has plenty of money to enjoy his privacy and a fancy apartment. What's the problem with that?"

"Thelma is generous in finding the good in people, but her visit with Sean left her uneasy. Once she mentioned she was considering moving to Golden Living, his interest in her finances took over the conversation."

"Thelma wants to move?" Jason's eyes opened wide and his jaw dropped.

"No." Annie waved her hands in front of herself, like she was waving away his shock. "It was only our plan to try to get information from Dawn, actually. We didn't even know Sean would jump into this conversation. And another thing. He had one corner of his apartment set up like an office with a couple of computers."

Jason leaned his head back and twisted it from side to side. "I'll humor you for a minute longer. How does

Sean fit into this money scam? Is he working alone or with others?"

"I know it all sounds kind of ridiculous but there is a connection. Forrest, the guy who was murdered, appeared to be friendly with Sean, at least according to Marvin." Annie held up her finger to keep Jason from interrupting. "And, Forrest negotiated a sale for Sylvia. She's desperate for money and she sold a family lithograph by Norman Rockwell. I saw it in Sean's apartment." She sat back and let out a big sigh.

"What you are telling me is that someone is scamming the folks that reside at Golden Living out of their savings." He tapped his reading glasses on the pile of papers. "You think there could be information in here to expose this scam. Forrest could be the common link but he got on the wrong side of whoever is running it and ended up dead."

Annie nodded her head vigorously. "Right. Is that so far-fetched?"

"Nope. But looking for that connection in these papers is going to be like looking for a needle in a haystack. The only hope is to get more information from Sylvia to see where her money actually went and then the police can take over. And find out what bank Golden Living uses."

"The other thing that has been bothering me is about Marvin. He always seems to be in the area, keeping an eye on the comings and goings whenever something happens. He hated Forrest and didn't seem to be upset at all that he's dead. I'm not sure I want him to be privy to anything we uncover. Just in case."

"Just in case he's the murderer?"

"Exactly. But then the rest of my theory connecting a money scam to the murder has no merit. I don't think Marvin is the type to force elders out on the street."

"Or he has you completely bamboozled. I think Marvin knows how to play someone to get what he wants. Be careful around him."

Jason stood and stretched. "Are we done for the night?"

"I think I'll take Roxy out for a short walk. Do you want to come?"

"Okay. It's a cool night. A good chance to clear my head from all this." He waved his hand over the papers on the table.

At the sound of her name, Roxy was off the couch and waiting at the door. Annie stuck her small flashlight in her pocket and pulled on a flannel shirt. Jason followed Annie and Roxy outside.

The spring air felt fresh and clean. Lights across the lake reflected on the water, making it look like stars twinkling on the choppy surface. A barred owl hoo-hooed in the distance. Annie slipped her hand into Jason's and matched her stride to his. Roxy dashed back and forth across the trail, following whatever smells her nose picked up.

"Do you really think Marvin could be the killer after the story he told us tonight?" Jason asked. "That incident from his working past shaped his life. Even if he hated Forrest, I think he has a stronger drive to protect people."

"I hope you're right. He's a quirky guy but I'm getting attached to him. I'd hate for him to be the killer, even if it was for what he thought were the right reasons."

The lights from the houses set back from the path were enough to illuminate the trail. When they got near Thelma's house, Annie was surprised to see it well lit up still. She nudged Jason with her elbow. "What do you think those three are up to?"

"Maybe Thelma's crossword puzzle? Wouldn't that be a gift to you?" He laughed. "Seriously, I wouldn't be surprised if they are discussing Sylvia's situation. If she is out of money and has to move, maybe they'll figure out a solution."

"Thelma doesn't beat around the bush, so you could be right. Maybe she'll offer Sylvia a room in her house. Thelma's son doesn't want her living alone and Sylvia could be good company."

They walked in silence for a few minutes. "Did I tell you that the murder weapon belonged to Sylvia?" Annie felt Jason's hand tighten around her fingers.

"No. That tidbit has been missing from the narrative." Jason sounded annoyed.

"And, she shot her husband in self-defense twenty years ago."

"Maybe she shot the Easter bunny because he tried to rob her apartment? Come on, Annie, you can't eliminate a possible suspect because you like them. When were you planning to tell me these important details?"

"You're right. Sylvia and Marvin need to be considered as suspects. I got sidetracked with the papers and Sylvia's financial predicament."

"I know you did, but that financial predicament put her in Dawn's office at the time of the murder. I think all this money stuff is a wild goose chase so you don't have to look at the facts which are staring you in the face about someone you like."

Annie knew Jason was at least partly correct. She didn't want Sylvia to be the murderer, but she had to consider that what she wanted might not be reality.

"Get Sylvia's financial information and find out more about her gun and her history. There isn't a rule that says a killer can't be dressed as a little old lady that wrings her hands and acts helpless. Don't forget that."

CHAPTER 18

Annie was happy she didn't have to get to the Black Cat Café first on Saturday morning. Leona had that responsibility squarely back on her shoulders.

The oldies station blasted when Annie opened the door after the sun was up. Leona sang and danced between the work island where she had the mixer set up and the oven which was already filling the café with mouthwatering aromas. Delicious cakes, moist muffins, crumbly scones, and juicy pies covered the counters. And, of course, plenty of Leona's special Easter hot cross buns were cooling on racks. It would be virtually impossible for anyone to enter and leave empty-handed with all the temptations on display.

Unless they ate their treats and put on blinders before leaving.

"You're full of energy this morning," Annie said as she tied on a red apron with black cats leaping in the air.

Leona turned the mixer off and pointed her wooden spoon at Annie. "Thanks to you. I haven't felt this refreshed in a long time. You and Jason should go away for a night or two."

"My thought exactly." But Annie's planning would have to wait.

Mia arrived, and the three women efficiently got the café ready for a holiday weekend rush.

Annie stocked the pastry display with warm-from-the-oven blueberry muffins, fruit tarts, individual lemon cakes, and Leona's own marshmallow Easter critters. Rich sour cream coffee cakes smothered with streusel topping and gooey custard-filled éclairs were ready to be added as soon as space was available. A special section was set up just for the dozens of hot cross buns that were sure to fly from the café.

With the addition of a vase with daffodils on each table and booth, Mia stood back and surveyed the café. "The coffee's ready and the drink cart is well stocked with a variety of teas, a bowl of freshly whipped cream, sugar, and hot chocolate mix." Her voice held pride.

With everything looking festive and smelling scrumptious, Annie fixed herself a coffee, sat down at the counter, and snagged a warm hot cross bun off the cooling rack while Leona's back was turned. "I hope we have enough for this weekend." She caught a bit of the sugar frosting with her tongue before it had a chance to drip on the counter.

"I hope we have enough for *today*," Leona said. "I'll be baking plenty more this afternoon *and* tomorrow morning. I have a pile of orders on my desk that still need to be boxed up for pickup today which will put a good dent in what I've already baked this morning."

She wiped her forehead with the back of her hand, leaving a faint trail of flour just below her hair. "I loved my little get-away but it's even better to be back!"

Annie washed the hot cross bun down with the rest of her coffee and unlocked the café door.

As if she had been waiting just outside for the sound of the lock, Martha pushed through, followed by Sylvia and Marvin. "Good morning ladies. It sure does smell scrumptious in here."

Marvin immediately made his way to the pastry display. He studied each tray before he looked at Annie. "I want that big hot cross bun that's all the way in the back. Got to get my money's worth."

Annie used a waxed sheet to reach in for the bun. "This one?" She knew they were all the same but if Marvin thought this one was bigger, she'd humor him.

He shook his head. "No, the one next to it. And I'll take two more in a bag to take with me. That one and that one." He pointed to one on the edge and another in the corner. "My mother, Peggy Sue, always made hot cross buns. Yours probably won't be as good as hers."

Annie suppressed a smile at Marvin's insult. It was part of his character, after all.

He took his plate and made himself comfortable in the same booth he sat in on Thursday.

Martha selected a blueberry muffin. "I know I should try something different but nothing ever seems to taste as good as Leona's blueberry muffins. And I know these just got baked this morning."

"A lot of people agree with you on that, Martha." Annie glanced at Marvin and saw he was busy eating his bun with a fork. She lowered her voice. "How was their night at Thelma's house? Did you get any details?"

"I didn't get all the details but Marvin complained about her guest bed. It was too soft, I think he might have moved to the floor; and he said all the branches on the trees kept banging against the house so he couldn't sleep. I don't think Thelma will invite him back again. Sylvia slept well but I have the feeling she's nervous about going back to her apartment. She insisted we stop here, not that I mind at all."

"She's only having coffee and nothing to eat?" Annie saw that Sylvia was sitting across from Marvin staring out the window with only a coffee in front of her.

"Give me another muffin for her. Maybe she doesn't want to spend the money."

Martha carried two plates to the booth and slid in next to Sylvia. Annie's attention was pulled away from that trio when Detective Christy Crank arrived at the pastry display. She definitely had her work look in place with her hair pulled into a tight bun.

"Oh my. There are more choices here than hairs on the Easter bunny. What do you recommend?"

Annie wondered if somehow that was a trick question. "Everyone loves the blueberry muffins, but Leona only makes these hot cross buns at Easter time."

"Hot cross buns, huh? I haven't had one of those since the last time I visited my grandmother. I'll take a half dozen."

"Since when did you develop such a big sweet tooth?" Annie knew Christy didn't carry an extra ounce on her petite frame.

"Oh, they aren't all for me. I'm heading to Golden Living and I'll share over there."

"Any new leads?" Annie asked without much expectation that Christy would share anything. She counted out the hot cross buns into a bag.

"Possibly. Do you know a guy named Sean that lives there?"

The hairs on Annie's neck rose. "Sean Woodman?"

"Yeah, that's his name."

"I met him yesterday, why?"

"He thinks someone might have broken into his apartment. He thinks something is missing." Christy took the bag and stared at Annie. "You were there yesterday, weren't you?"

"I brought my neighbor, Thelma Dodd, over to visit with a couple of her friends. Sean was someone she knew when they were younger."

"And she was in his apartment?"

"Yes. Sean invited her in." Annie had no intention of admitting she was also in Sean's apartment unless she had to. Was she on Sean's radar as the thief?

"How about you? Did you go in, too?"

"Roxy and I went in to get Thelma when I finished visiting with some other people. They had a muffin and then Thelma, Roxy, and I left. He wasn't very friendly."

Christy laughed. "Tell me about it. I hope one of these buns will soften him up a bit. He probably just misplaced what he thinks he lost but I have to go through the motions."

"How about the other, ah, event? Any more leads there?"

"Nice try. We're following everything that turns up but you know I can't give you any details." Christy started to walk away.

"Christy? Have you heard any complaints about how Golden Living is run? How they manage their payments and that kind of thing?"

"That's an interesting question. There has been some chatter, why?"

"I think it could be related to the," Annie mouthed the word 'murder', "Wednesday night."

"The victim didn't live at Golden Living." Christy's eyes scrunched up like she was trying hard to make a connection. "Do you know something you should be telling me?"

"Nothing concrete, but there does appear to be overlap that I find is more than coincidence."

"Let's talk more about this when you aren't working. I've got to run now." Christy chatted with Leona when she paid and took a detour to the table where Martha, Sylvia, and Marvin were finishing their coffees before she left the café.

Martha ushered Sylvia and Marvin out the door and returned to the pastry display alone. "I'll take a half dozen blueberry muffins to go. I think Sylvia will need something to cheer her up after the detective's little visit."

"What happened?" Annie had been dying to ask Martha what Christy's chat was about but hadn't had a second of free time. She counted out the blueberry muffins into a bag for Martha and listened to the ominous warning.

"She was friendly, probably too friendly in my opinion. She wanted to check if Sylvia would be back at her apartment for," Martha put her fingers up in quotes, "a few questions. Of course, Sylvia is more nervous than a bunny in a wide open field surrounded by a fox family wondering what questions are coming at her."

"You can keep her company all day?" Annie asked.

"That's my plan. And Marvin, with all his complaining and weirdness, actually patted Sylvia's hand. I think those two are developing an odd friendship."

"Good. I'd rather have Marvin on my side than sneaking around behind my back. As soon as the rush is over here, I'll swing by Golden Living with Thelma and Roxy. I have a few questions to ask too, and I don't think Dawn Cross will like them."

CHAPTER 19

Annie jammed as much as possible into the pastry display, boxed up all the telephone orders, and, at the last minute, decided to bring a coconut layer cake with lemon curd filling with her. No one *needed* more sweets but that didn't mean they wouldn't *want* more.

Roxy managed to drag herself off the couch when Annie got home. "Is all the socializing wearing you out?" Annie asked her loyal companion. "We aren't done yet." She jotted her stuffed zucchini recipe on an index card in case she bumped into Gloria, pocketed a handful of dog biscuits, grabbed Roxy's leash, and got back in her car with Roxy for the short ride to Thelma's house.

Annie didn't know if Thelma would be up for another visit to Golden Living or would prefer to sit in her peaceful screened-in porch with a cup of tea working on her crossword puzzle. Annie hoped she was up for another visit because Thelma was her in to get into Dawn's office and ask some important questions.

Annie knocked on Thelma's door. There was no answer so she turned the knob quietly and poked her head in, wondering if Thelma might be taking her afternoon doze in her comfy chair. Roxy darted through the partially opened door before Annie could stop her.

"Hello, Roxy. Did you figure out how to open the door or is Annie with you?"

"I'm here, Thelma. Are you up for visitors?" Annie found Roxy with her head on Thelma's knee and Thelma's hand stroking Roxy's head.

"Can you pour some tea and sit down for a bit? I have some interesting information from last night's conversations."

Annie turned on the kettle, found the tray with tea cups, and listened to Thelma talk to Roxy. She could use some company, and after seeing her the night before with Smokey and Snowball curled in her lap, Annie had an idea.

"You know, Thelma," Annie said as she carried the tray into the porch, "I've been thinking that Snowball might like to be back in a home where he can get spoiled without any competition. He was an only cat where he came from, and he's adjusted okay to living with Roxy and Smokey, but he might be happier with you." Annie handed Thelma her tea.

"He is a super friendly cat and he would make it a bit less lonely here if you think he would like the change."

Annie nodded. "I think he'd love to keep you company and not have to share a lap with another cat."

"Okay then. Bring him over sometime and we'll give it a try." She took a dog treat from the jar next to her table and held it out for Roxy who took it gently. "Last night was interesting."

"Martha told me that Marvin had a few complaints."

Thelma chuckled. "He did, but he's harmless and he doesn't bother me. Sylvia, on the other hand, is the one I'm worried about."

"Oh?"

"Don't get me wrong, Annie. I don't think she killed that young man but I think she might be in danger. What with all the clues pointing in her direction, it seems that someone is out to get her out of the way. I have to get back to see that manager and find out what her angle is. "

Annie was happy to hear that Thelma was up for another visit with Dawn Cross. "Did Sylvia talk to you about her finances at all?"

"Only the same thing you already told me about losing her apartment at the end of the month. I don't know how that could happen." She shook her head with disbelief.

"Well, I don't either, but if I can get ahold of her bank statements, I might be able to check them for discrepancies against the paperwork I took yesterday, which means another trip to Golden Living. Are you coming with me today?" Annie stood.

A grin spread across Thelma's face. "What kind of question is that? Of course I'm coming. Who knows, you'll probably need another diversion. I think the three of us—Roxy, you, and I—are the tricky trio. Who at Golden Living would suspect a therapy dog, a beautiful young woman, and a little old retired school teacher to be working on uncovering a scam?"

Annie laughed. "You, Thelma Dodd, are one of a kind." She helped Thelma to her walker and they made their way outside to Annie's car.

"What's in that Black Cat Café box?" Thelma pointed to the box on the passenger seat before Annie picked it up and set it in Thelma's lap after she sat down.

"A surprise weapon—to be used in an emergency, or to bribe someone for information."

Thelma opened the box. "Oh my. This is one of my favorites, coconut cake with lemon filling. How do you stay so slim working around all the delicious pastries? I'd eat up all the profits and then I wouldn't fit through the door."

"I do sample the goods but I don't have time to eat too many. Plus, Leona runs a tight ship. I had to sneak this out when she wasn't looking."

"That makes it all the more tempting. I hope Sylvia can enjoy a piece. She didn't eat a thing this morning before she left. She said her stomach was in knots."

"Martha bought her a blueberry muffin, but I don't know if she ate it or if Marvin did. His sweet tooth is a bottomless pit."

When Annie reached the center of town, a siren sounded behind her and she pulled her car to the side as an ambulance raced by.

"I wonder where he's off to," Thelma said as she tried to hide the worried look on her face.

As Annie pulled into the Golden Living parking lot, they didn't have to wonder for long. The ambulance was parked at the front entrance. She had a bad feeling as she saw Detective Christy Crank close the ambulance door and say something to Martha.

Annie had to wait for several long minutes until the ambulance left. A spot was open near the entrance and she took no time parking there.

"What's going on?" Annie asked Martha as soon as she was out of her car.

"Sylvia fainted and hit her head on the wall. She probably has a concussion." Martha twisted her hands together. "I should have seen it coming. She didn't eat anything all day and said she wasn't feeling well."

"What was Detective Crank doing here?" Annie glanced at her car to check on Thelma who had her door open and her feet on the ground.

"She had questions for Sylvia but it never even got that far. Sylvia took one look at the detective in the doorway and down she went."

Annie got Thelma's walker and helped her out of the car. Roxy jumped from the back seat to the front and stayed close to Thelma as she maneuvered toward the entrance of Golden Living. Annie almost forgot the cake but ran back to the car and grabbed it.

"I've got Sylvia's keys so we can go to her apartment," Martha said, leading the way.

Annie's mind raced. Should she search Sylvia's apartment for her financial statements or wait until Sylvia returned?

"Mrs. Dodd, you must be feeling better." Dawn stepped from her office and put her arm around Thelma. "Would you care to continue our conversation from yesterday?"

"Yes, of course, but first I'm having tea and coconut cake with my friend."

Dawn's smile stayed frozen on her face. "What friend would that be?"

"Hurry up," Marvin shouted from down the hall. "What's taking you so long?"

Dawn's eyes flickered to Marvin. She leaned close to Thelma. "Be careful around that one, he really can't be trusted."

"You don't say. I'll have to count my silverware when I get home and see whether he stole anything last night." Thelma turned away from Dawn and headed straight for Marvin. Annie heard a quiet twitter come from Thelma.

Once they were all safely inside Sylvia's apartment, Thelma said, "You know who can't be trusted? Someone that tries to stir up fear with vague statements. I'm more determined than ever to find out what that Dawn is up to. What can we do Annie?"

"I'll look through Sylvia's desk to see what I can find. I don't think she'll mind." Annie pulled a drawer of Sylvia's desk out and began a methodical search through the papers.

Martha had the tea kettle heating up.

Marvin eyed the Black Cat Café box. "What's in there?"

"Haven't you had enough sweets today?" Martha scolded. "You finished your other two hot cross buns on the way here."

"But that was this morning. I could use a little pick-me-up with the tea."

Annie found a stack of bank statements neatly clipped together with a paper clip. "This might be just what I need." She sat at Sylvia's table and quickly scanned the withdrawals. "Right here." She underlined an entry with her finger. "This looks suspicious—fifty thousand dollars transferred just a week ago." She flipped some more pages. "Another one a week before for ten thousand dollars." Annie looked at Martha. "Do you have any explanation for this? Did Sylvia talk to you about her finances?"

Martha shook her head. "She only mentioned that her bank balance was dwindling but she didn't say why or ask me for any advice."

"Marvin. It's time for you to share some of your secrets." Annie opened the cake box and cut a big slice. "Cake for information. It's your choice."

He reached for the plate. "I don't know about any money transfers, but I do know that Shady Sean spends time in Dawn's office at night." He took a forkful of cake, chewed, and swallowed. "When he thinks no one is watching."

Thelma finished her tea.

Marvin had a second piece of cake.

Roxy kept her head on Thelma's knee.

Annie and Martha studied Sylvia's papers.

"Maybe it's time to head over to see Dawn. Are you coming with me, Annie?" Thelma asked.

"Yes. Then we should make a stop in Sean's apartment, too. Martha, are you going to the hospital to check on Sylvia? I think someone should stay with her, especially if Detective Crank starts asking her questions."

"I'll go too," Marvin said. "We can take turns so she's never alone." He looked at the three women.

"That's an excellent idea, Marvin," Martha said.

"Should we bring her some cake?"

Annie cut a couple of pieces and hunted around for foil. As a last resort, she opened the dishwasher to see if there was a clean container. She didn't find what she expected but what met her eyes made her laugh. "I guess Sylvia's dishwasher is broken?"

Martha leaned over Annie's shoulder. "Huh. I guess you must be right but she's resourceful by using it for storage."

Annie took the foil out of the broken dishwasher and wrapped the cake. "Marvin, don't forget to keep your ears and eyes alert at the hospital. If the detective shows up to ask questions, be sure to interrupt and tell her some of your interesting discoveries from your wanderings around here. I want her to start thinking that Forrest's murder is connected to how Dawn runs this place."

Marvin grinned. "I can do that. And then I'll entertain her with how beans don't agree with me."

"Good." Annie handed him the wrapped cake. "Remember, this is for Sylvia, not you."

"What if she doesn't want it?"

"No wonder you can't sleep at night and you wander all over this place. You eat too much sugar," Annie scolded.

Thelma stood, Roxy stayed at her side, and they all left Sylvia's apartment to gather more information.

CHAPTER 20

As Annie and Thelma approached Dawn's office, the unmistakable sound of an argument drifted to her ears. Annie stopped dead in her tracks and held her hand out to stop Thelma while they were still out of view but within hearing distance.

"I found her first," hissed Gloria. "The rule is that whoever signs a new tenant gets the commission."

"You're right. Whoever *signs* a new tenant, not whoever *talks* to a potential new tenant," Dawn replied, her voice calm and measured.

"And what do you think the sly detective will think when I tell her you were still in the building when the Easter bunny met his maker?" Gloria said with an unmistakable hint of hatred.

Annie felt her mouth open and she looked at Thelma who was equally shocked.

"And how would you know that unless you were still here too, you fool. We have to keep our stories straight and let Sylvia take the fall. All the pieces are falling into place very nicely. Now, stay out of my way with Thelma Dodd and you can have the next one." Annie couldn't see Dawn's expression but she could imagine that she had an evil glint in her eye.

They were running out of time to help Sylvia.

A door slammed between Dawn and Gloria's offices. Annie took Thelma's elbow and they rounded the corner into Dawn's office. Dawn stood with her back to the door and one hand rubbed her neck.

"Is this a bad time?" Annie asked in her friendliest voice.

Dawn whirled around. "Oh, I didn't hear you come in. I guess my mind was on something else."

Dawn's mind certainly *was* on something else—how to steal Thelma's money as quickly as possible, Annie guessed. She hoped Dawn didn't suspect that her private and controversial conversation with Gloria might have been overheard.

Dawn held her hand out toward a chair. "Please. Have a seat, Thelma. Are you going to the sunroom with your therapy dog, Annie?"

Annie helped Thelma get settled in the chair. Roxy took up her position next to Thelma, Annie pulled another chair close to Thelma, and sat next to them. "No. I'll stay here with Thelma."

Dawn frowned and sat behind her desk. Her fingers flicked through several folders. She pulled one out and opened it. Annie could see Thelma's name written in big black letters at the top. "I've taken the liberty of getting you into the system and now, to reserve a spot, all I'll need is your signature." She held a paper.

"Before we get to that," Annie leaned slightly forward, "do you have any word on how Sylvia May is doing? We," she glanced at Thelma, "were shocked when we got here to find out that she was in the ambulance."

"Sylvia? No, I haven't heard anything. Why don't we—"

"What was Detective Crank doing at her apartment?"

"I suppose she had questions about the murder."

Annie's hand covered her mouth. "Sweet Sylvia? She's a suspect?"

Dawn put the paper she was holding down. "You didn't know? The gun you found?"

Annie nodded.

"It belonged to Sylvia. Of course, she made up some story about how it had gone missing but she never reported it, so..." Dawn shrugged.

"I would never have guessed." Annie didn't dare look at Thelma anymore or she knew she wouldn't be able to keep up the fake surprise reactions to everything Dawn said.

"So, you see, that's why we'll have an opening for you, Thelma." Dawn smiled and picked up the paper again.

"You're saying Sylvia's not just a suspect but you think she's the murderer and won't be coming back here to Golden Living?" Annie hoped her face conveyed the appropriate shock.

"Well, I don't know for a *fact*, but don't you agree that it's awfully suspicious that her gun is the murder weapon? And then she fainted at the sight of the detective? What do *you* think?"

Annie leaned back in her chair. "But she was in the closet, hiding, at the time of the murder. How could she kill Forrest while she was hiding in the closet *and* find time to stash the gun?"

Dawn flicked her wrist. "Are you serious? The fact that she was even in my office was odd. She and I had already had our little chat about her apartment. Why did she come back a second time?" Dawn leaned across her desk and lowered her voice. "I think she followed Forrest into my office, shot him, and then hid in the closet until you found her." She sat back with a satisfied look as if she'd wrapped up a present all nice and tidy.

"Why would she kill Forrest? She liked him." Annie tilted her head and scrunched her brow.

"She wanted...oh, I don't have *all* the answers. Who knows why anyone does anything? Now let's—"

Thelma put her hand up as if she was asking permission to speak. "My friend Sean told me that

Sylvia had to move because she was out of money. I didn't think it had anything to do with that poor boy who was murdered."

"You're friends with Sean Woodman?" The color in Dawn's face turned to a washed out shade of gray.

What did that mean? Was Dawn afraid of Sean for some reason?

Thelma stood. "I think I'm done here. I'm not sure I like the way you treat those in your care."

"Wait, Mrs. Dodd. Thelma." Dawn was at Thelma's side easing her back into the chair. "I'm sure we can work something out. You've got the wrong impression of Golden Living." She closed her door. "I rarely make an offer so generous, but if you sign today, I'll give you a big discount."

Thelma winked at Annie while Dawn's back was turned. "I'm listening."

"Okay." Dawn spread papers out so both Thelma and Annie could see. "Right here," Dawn used her pen to circle a number, "is our usual price for the apartment that will be available." She crossed that number out and scribbled a much lower number before she looked at Thelma and smiled. "It's a fantastic deal, but I can't hold the opening. You have to sign now or lose it."

"Oh, I don't know." Thelma hemmed and hawed.

"This is how it works. With your signature today, it reserves a spot and you agree to sign over your property to Golden Living. Of course, we only use a portion of the money for the buy in and the rest will fund the monthly payments for as long as you live here." Dawn smiled and pushed the paper closer to Thelma.

Thelma picked up a pen. She chewed on the top. "That money will be in an account for me?"

Dawn nodded. "It's all spelled out at the bottom. Right here." She pointed to a paragraph of tiny print.

"In my name?"

"Along with Golden Living."

Thelma looked at Annie. "What do you think?"

Dawn's jaw clenched. This was why she tried to get Annie to leave. Dawn knew it would be harder to get a signature while Thelma had someone else to bounce the decision off of.

"Well. It's all very interesting, Thelma." Annie shuffled the papers together. "I think you should have your son advise you on this. He's the one who thinks you shouldn't be living alone."

Dawn tried to grab the papers back from Annie but she couldn't quite reach them once Annie sat back in her chair. She safely slid the papers into Thelma's big bag. "Do you have any more questions for Dawn?"

"I think I have enough to think about for now." Thelma stood. "Oh, yes, one more question. How often do you have robberies here? I don't want to have to worry about my valuables."

Annie wondered what, if any, *valuables* Thelma was referring to or, more likely, Thelma was on a fishing trip.

"Robberies? Oh heavens, no. Golden Living is safe and secure."

"Sylvia said your safe was cleaned out when that poor boy was murdered. I wondered if that was the whole motive. What was stolen? Money?"

"I don't think you can believe what Sylvia said, now can you?" Dawn spread her arms out with a gesture that she wasn't hiding anything. "After all, why would the police have her as a suspect?"

"So, nothing was stolen?" Good for Thelma. She wasn't letting Dawn get away answering a question with a question.

Dawn shuffled the papers on her desk. "Something from the safe is missing but I'm positive it will turn up."

"Oh, I hope so because Sylvia told me that you keep a lot of cash in your safe which seems kind of reckless." Thelma kept her gaze on Dawn.

"Oh, haha. She must have been referring to the deposit that went to the bank that day. I like to have cash on hand in case anyone needs a bit of help. It's easier than getting them to the bank sometimes. They write a check to Golden Living and I give them the cash. I can assure you that all the money is safe and sound at the Catfish Credit Union."

"Wonderful. I'll be back in touch after I have my son look everything over. He's an accountant, by the way, and he'll probably have more questions for you." Thelma turned to Annie. "Seany is expecting us, we'd better go now."

Annie didn't miss the muscle spasm in the corner of Dawn's eye as she shifted the Black Cat Café cake box from her lap to her arm. This conversation had not gone the way Dawn had hoped.

CHAPTER 21

Roxy was happy to be moving again as Annie and Thelma headed down the bright tiled hallway toward Sean Woodman's apartment.

"Do you think this cake will be a good enough bribe to get us inside his apartment?" Annie asked Thelma.

"I'll get us in. Don't worry. The cake will just be an extra reward."

Annie knocked on Sean's apartment door and waited. "Maybe he's not here." She knocked again.

Just as Annie was about to check the sunroom to see if Sean was sitting in his corner, the door opened. His wheelchair blocked them from entering. "I'm busy."

"Oh, Seany. I really need to talk to you about moving to Golden Living. You were always so good with numbers, and the information Dawn gave me just doesn't make much sense." Thelma cocked her head and raised her eyebrows. "Are you sure you can't spare a few minutes?"

The muscles in Sean's jaw clenched but he moved his wheelchair out of the way. "Come in then."

"Annie has cake, too. Can you make us tea?"

"Are you serious, Thelma?"

"Yes, I am. She has coconut cake with lemon curd filling. If I remember correctly, you love lemon. Am I right?" Thelma made her way into Sean's apartment and sat in a chair at his table.

Annie and Roxy followed and she put the cake box on his table. She sensed some anger behind Sean's words and decided it was smart to just let Thelma handle the visit as she felt was best.

"I do love lemon," Sean admitted. "I have coffee already made. That will have to do." He got out three cups, not giving a choice in the drink department.

Annie moved Thelma's walker off to one side. With her back to Sean, she tried her best to see what was on his computer screen but it was only numbers that made no sense to her.

She opened her cake box.

"Plates are over there," he pointed to a cabinet. "And forks are here," he slid a drawer open.

Annie carried the plates and forks to the table where Sean already had the coffee, sugar, and cream. She cut three pieces, handing one to Martha and then Sean before she sat with her own piece.

"Now, tell me what Dawn offered you."

"How do you know she made an offer, Seany?" Thelma sipped her coffee but kept her eyes on Sean over the rim of her cup.

Sean sighed with exasperation. "Dawn always makes an offer. Especially when she thinks she has a customer with plenty of money. I've done some background checking on you Thelma—"

"You what? Are you working with Dawn?" Thelma's cup clattered on the saucer and almost tipped over.

"Working with her on what?" Sean's eyes went between Annie and Thelma. "That's an odd question."

"Well, it's odd that you would do a background check on me, Seany. All you have to do is ask. Don't go doing a sneaky-peeky thing."

"I'm looking out for your welfare, Thelma. I've learned that Dawn has a habit of, let's just say, not being up front about everything she tells prospective new residents. The more information I have about your finances, the better I can help you get the best deal from her." He looked directly at Thelma. "I want to help you."

"Oh." Thelma's eyes cut to the side to look at Annie. Thelma managed a quick eyebrow wiggle while Sean was focused on his piece of cake. This was an unexpected direction and could mean exactly what Sean was saying about helping, or he could be in cahoots with Dawn. Or, did he have something else up his sleeve?

"In that case," Annie finally found her voice, "are there set rates for apartments or does she throw out numbers to pull new residents in?"

Sean savored another forkful of the coconut cake. "I'm not privy to what offers she makes, but I do know that prices that people actually buy in with are all over the place."

"And how about Sylvia's situation? She's been told her money is running out and she'll have to move. Does this happen often?"

"Unfortunately, it does. That's why I want to look out for Thelma's money."

Annie leaned toward Sean. "Exactly what do you mean by *looking out for her money*? Do you intend to manage it for her?"

"What? I told you yesterday I try to stay out of other people's business but, for old time's sake, I don't want to see Thelma get taken advantage of. I can give her sound advice."

Annie ate some cake and drank some coffee. She didn't know what Sean's game was and she wasn't sure what to ask next. This was all so unexpected.

She gathered her thoughts and decided to get some concrete answers. "Why do you have Sylvia's Norman Rockwell lithograph? You and Forrest were working together to take advantage of people here?"

Sean's nostrils flared. "I'm not sure inviting you in was a good idea. This is exactly why I don't get involved with other people. With all the rumors and misinformation that's spread around here, it's enough to make me lock the door and never leave again."

Annie sat back. "Well, how about you tell us what's really going on, then. Shed some light on why people like Sylvia are running out of money, why you and Forrest appeared to have some kind of friendship and," Annie stared at Sean, "why you go into Dawn's office at night."

Sean pushed back from the table. He maneuvered his wheelchair expertly through his sparsely-furnished apartment and opened a locked cabinet.

Okay, this was creepy, Annie thought. Roxy was on her feet watching Sean's movements. What was he planning to do? Annie pushed back from the table, ready to stand and flee if necessary. Thelma put her hand on Annie's arm and shook her head.

"Maybe you can help me after all." He returned to the table with a notebook. "I did buy Sylvia's lithograph, but not for the reason you think. I plan to return it to her. And I did get friendly with Forrest, but again, not for the reason you think. Forrest had a scheming mind and all he cared about was schmoozing up to the vulnerable people here, find out what they had of value, and giving them pennies for it when they were short of money. By letting him *think* I liked him, I would buy those valuables for safe keeping. Forrest was never happy with the amount of money I gave him but he had no other option to unload anything for a quick turnover of cash in his pocket." He held up the notebook. "It's all in here."

Annie blinked. "I need another cup of coffee."

Sean actually smiled. "Bring the whole pot over. We'll all need it."

Thelma patted his arm. "You've really surprised me, Seany. In a good way."

"Thelma?" Sean said.

"Yes, Seany?"

"Please stop calling me Seany. I hate it."

Thelma smiled and nodded.

Annie refilled everyone's cup with the remaining coffee and sliced more cake. She even remembered she had dog treats in her pocket for Roxy.

"Okay. The cake is gone. Let's get to work," Sean said. "Now that I know I can trust the two of you, maybe we can finally unravel what's happening here and clean this place up so good people don't have all their hard-earned money stolen from under their noses."

"How did you decide you could trust us?" Annie asked. She still wasn't one-hundred percent sure she could trust Sean.

"When you told me that Sylvia was being forced out, I got furious and decided whoever is behind what's going on had to be stopped. You were so concerned about her, I suspected you might dig into what was going on. Am I right?"

Annie nodded.

"But when Thelma said she was meeting with Dawn, I got worried. Worried about *you*, Thelma. Showing up today with your questions made me realize I had to get someone to help me put everything together before someone else got hurt...or killed...and the coconut cake with lemon curd filling didn't hurt." Another rare smile softened Sean's face.

"Do you know who killed Forrest?" Annie asked.

"That little weasel? I don't really care. He got exactly what he deserved."

"I think it's connected to the money scam going on here," Annie said.

"I didn't think of that. He was always involved in a lot of little deals. I didn't think he was smart enough to carry out stealing big chunks of money."

"Well, maybe he wasn't involved, but he might have known who was," Annie suggested. "That information could have gotten him killed."

Sean nodded. "He did have a habit of sticking his nose where it wasn't wanted." He looked at Annie. "Kind of like you. I thought you were in cahoots with the management when you first showed up. You'd better be extra careful who you rub the wrong way."

"Yeah. I hear that a lot." Annie looked at Sean's computer set-up. "Golden Living uses the Catfish Credit Union. Is there any way to see if they've made big deposits lately?"

"I'm good with hacking but I'm not sure I can crack the security of a bank. What else do you have?"

Annie put Sylvia's financial statements on the table. "How about this? Is there any way to see where these big deposits ended up?" Annie pointed to the large amounts that had been recently withdrawn from her account.

Sean quickly skimmed the documents. "Holy Toledo. Someone left quite a trail. Do you think Sylvia will give me permission to access her account? I'll need her log in information and password."

"She's in the hospital," Thelma told Sean. "She fell and has a concussion."

"Oh. I'll play around and see what I can find. I have her account number so that's a start." Sean pushed away from the table. "I'll get started on this now."

A loud knock sounded on Sean's door. He checked the time. "It's probably my dinner getting delivered. I don't eat at the dining hall."

He opened the door and a young woman wearing a Golden Living shirt smiled at Sean. "Your dinner, Mr. Woodman. And a delivery from the pharmacy."

"Thank you, Sally. What's on the menu tonight?"

"I'm not sure you'll like it, sir. The weekend chef forgot you're a vegetarian so you won't want the entrée, but there's a delicious salad loaded with spinach, avocado, cranberries, and tomato, plus risotto and applesauce."

"I'll be fine. It's not the first time this has happened." Sean took the tray and closed the door.

"That's a nice service," Annie said as Sean wheeled himself back to the table.

"You get what you pay for, I've discovered. I give Sally a little extra to bring my dinner to me."

"She doesn't work seven days, does she?"

"Unfortunately, no. On her days off I rely on Dawn or Gloria to deliver my meal. They usually remember." He shrugged. "I always have something on hand if a meal doesn't show up."

Annie's phone beeped with a text message. "It's from Martha," she said as she tapped the screen on her phone. "This doesn't sound good. Detective Crank is hanging around waiting to question Sylvia."

CHAPTER 22

Thelma decided she should go home and get some rest since there wasn't anything she'd be able to help Sylvia with at the moment. After Annie brought Thelma to her house, she dropped Roxy at home so she wouldn't be stuck in the car at the hospital for who knew how long. Plus, she wanted to see Jason.

As soon as she stepped inside, the wonderful aroma of garlic hit her nose. The table was set for two with exactly what she expected the night before if she hadn't ended up with last minute guests.

Jason leaned over the table, lighting two tall white tapers. "Good. You didn't bring anyone extra tonight." His warm smile melted her heart, and when his arms circled her body, Annie fell right into his strong embrace.

"What are you cooking? As soon as my nose got a whiff, my stomach reminded me to send down something delicious."

"Nothing too fancy—pesto and fresh linguine with a salad. Would you like a glass of wine first?"

Annie hesitated. She knew Martha was expecting her at the hospital, but would it be horrible if she relaxed for an hour with Jason?

"Your non-answer is telling me that something has come up." He held Annie at arm's length and waited for a reply.

"It's Sylvia. She fell at Golden Living and is at the hospital. Martha went over there about an hour ago and I suppose I should go see what's going on. She's expecting me."

"You don't sound especially sure about that."

"I'll take that glass of wine, eat dinner, and head over later. I doubt there is anything I can do for her now, anyway."

Jason smiled. "Going now or waiting for an hour or so won't matter." He poured two glasses of wine and handed one to Annie.

"I like that idea." She sat on the couch while Jason heated water for the linguine. "Thelma and I made a new friend today."

"At Golden Living?"

"Yup. Actually, it turns out that Sean, who I told you about last night?"

Jason nodded.

"Well, he's a good guy after all."

"Wasn't he in on buying that artwork from Sylvia through the murder victim?"

"Yes, but he's planning to return it to Sylvia. He is trying to figure out what's going on at Golden Living and who is stealing money from some of the residents."

"About that," Jason said. "I looked over the papers you took from Dawn's office and they appear to be balance amounts for different accounts. And the paper you took from Sean," Jason looked up from draining the linguine. "Does he know you stole something from him?"

"Ah, no. I'm not touching that issue for now."

"Anyway, that paper from his apartment matches one of the papers from Dawn's office. I think he might be copying her papers."

"Why?"

"If there is something illegal going on, he can compare the numbers over time and see when someone's account drops too quickly. That's my guess." Jason carried a big bowl of pasta with pesto to the table and set it alongside his salad. "Ready to eat?"

"Definitely." Annie hoped the meal would revive her diminishing energy level so she could be focused when she went to the hospital.

Jason stood behind Annie's chair and slid it in after she was settled. He topped off her glass of wine and served her a scoop of pesto pasta. "Help yourself to the salad." He walked around the table, sat, and filled his own plate. He raised his glass. "Cheers. Enjoy this break in your search for answers."

Annie clinked her glass against Jason's. "To a break, so my mind can come back stronger than before."

The candle glow and soft tinkle of forks on plates had a calming effect that surprised Annie. With her last mouthful of pasta and final sip of wine, she leaned back and sighed with contentment. "Do you think I should trust Sean Woodman? Or do you think he could be playing me for a fool?"

"That's a tough question, Annie. What does your gut tell you?"

"To trust him. Everything he said made sense except when we talked about Forrest. Sean didn't mince words when he told us that Forrest got exactly what he deserved. I can't rule out that Sean could be trying to uncover the money problems and also be the killer."

Jason wiped his mouth and lined up his fork and knife on the edge of his plate. "Let's walk through how he might have had the opportunity. He made it clear he didn't like Forrest, but let's start with how he could have gotten Sylvia's gun."

"Okay. Here's my theory on that. Forrest conned a lot of the residents with his charm and Sylvia definitely liked him. She needed money and sold her Norman Rockwell lithograph so maybe she approached Forrest about selling her gun, too. Sean ended up with the lithograph, is it much of a stretch that he bought the gun also?"

"That does make sense. So, Sean had a motive, means, but what about opportunity?"

Annie leaned forward. The food gave her a new burst of energy. "This was interesting. When Thelma and I were about to leave, Sean's dinner was delivered."

Jason raised his eyebrows but didn't make a comment.

"He told us that whenever this employee, Sally, was working, she would bring his dinner since he doesn't eat in the cafeteria. When I catered the Easter dinner, Gloria took Sean's meal and said she'd leave it on her desk for him to pick up."

Jason nodded. "I see where you're going with this. Sean had to go to her office to pick up his own meal that night and he could have shot Forrest at the same time. But wouldn't someone have seen him?"

"If Sean went into Gloria's office, he could have gone through the common door between her office and Dawn's. Sylvia said she heard someone coming down the hall so she hid in the closet. What if Sean happened to be following Forrest but went into Gloria's office for his dinner then checked to see what Forrest was doing?"

"I'm with you so far."

"He saw Forrest getting ready to rob the safe, shot him, took the money himself, went back through Gloria's office and into the bathroom next to her office where he dumped the gun."

"You never saw him?"

"No, but once I went into Dawn's office and found Sylvia, Sean could have left the bathroom and gotten back to his apartment."

"So, where's the money?"

"Dawn said she made a deposit that day at the Catfish Credit Union. Somehow, we have to find out if that happened or not." Annie leaned back in her chair. She was tired but satisfied with her theory.

"I have to give you credit, Annie, it sounds plausible."

"But, I have no evidence. I have to ask Marvin if he saw Sean that night."

"Don't forget, Sean had a reason to be in Gloria's office to pick up his dinner. He might have gotten his tray and left. Without more concrete evidence, the police won't act on your theory."

"I know. There's something else, though. Detective Crank told me Sean thinks someone broke into his apartment and took something. She wouldn't tell me what. Maybe Dawn was looking to get her money back."

While those thoughts settled between them, Jason cleared the plates while Annie covered the leftovers and stored them in the refrigerator. "Any dessert?"

Jason smiled. "I saved the best for last. Go sit down and close your eyes."

Annie heard plates sliding across the table. She smelled chocolate. Her mouth watered.

"Okay. You can look now."

A fudgy brownie covered with a dollop of cream, sliced strawberries, and a drizzle of hot fudge sauce teased her eyes. "Oh my," she moaned.

"Take a bite," Jason said with a big smile on his face.

"You aren't having one?"

He held up a second fork. "I'm hoping you'll share with me."

Annie laughed. "Only if you come sit next to me on the couch."

"Deal." Jason carried the plate. Annie tucked her legs under herself and leaned against Jason's side. "Here. You have the first bite." She held a forkful of deliciousness and Jason happily obeyed her.

It didn't take long for the brownie to disappear. "What a wonderful dinner you surprised me with, Jason Hunter. Thank you."

Jason took the plate away from Annie and set it on the coffee table. He put his arm around her shoulders and pulled her close. "You're welcome, Mrs. Hunter." He kissed the top of her head. "Are you still going to the hospital to check on Sylvia?"

"I can think of something I'd *rather* do, but I *should* go." Annie felt relaxed and comfortable, but letting Sylvia's problems return front and center in her mind made her anxious to get going.

"Right. I'll clean up the dishes, take Roxy out, and wait here for you."

Annie put several of Jason's fudge brownies in a bag in case Marvin was still at the hospital. They weren't the cream cheese brownies he requested and he would probably complain. Marvin managed to complain about anything and everything that he could think of, but he would gladly devour the sweets anyway.

When Annie arrived at the hospital parking lot, she texted Martha to find out where to meet up with her.

Annie heard back immediately, *Marvin and I are in the cafeteria.* That was easy. She followed the signs and found Martha and Marvin sitting at a table at the far side of the room.

"Did you bring anything for us? The food here is inedible," Marvin said as he poked at a sandwich of questionable ingredients sitting on a plate in front of him. "This is supposed to be turkey but it has no flavor at all. The bread is stale and the lettuce is rotten. Geesh." He spied the bag Annie held. "What's in the bag?"

"First, tell me how Sylvia is doing."

Martha's face was drawn and pale. "Not well. She had a seizure and hasn't been able to communicate. I'm really worried about her, Annie. And Detective Crank is hanging around."

"What's Christy here for?" Annie's relaxing hour and a half at home was suddenly a distant memory.

"I don't know, but she keeps checking with the doctor to find out when she can go in and ask Sylvia some questions."

Annie stood. She handed the bag to Marvin. "I brought brownies."

"Are you leaving already?" Martha's voice was panicked.

"I'm leaving the cafeteria to find Christy. She must know something about Forrest's murder that points to Sylvia but I think she's heading in the completely wrong direction."

"Sylvia's in room two-twenty-three. Good luck. I'm taking Marvin back to Golden Living soon and heading home to get some rest. I'll see you tomorrow."

Annie barely heard Martha's words because her eyes were focused on the detective waiting at the coffee machine.

Here goes nothing, she told herself. Somehow, she had to convince Christy to expand her investigation into Golden Living's finances. At least, get her to follow the money to see if the trail led to Forrest's murder.

CHAPTER 23

"Fancy meeting you here," Annie said as Detective Christy Crank turned around with her coffee.

"Annie Hunter, I could say the same thing. You always pop up like an unwanted nightmare during my investigations. What brings you to this unlikely hangout?" Christy sipped her coffee. "Nothing like delicious, watered-down dishwater that comes out of these machines. Aren't you having any?"

"No thanks. How is Sylvia?" Annie didn't know the best way to get Christy talking, but obviously, they both were at the hospital because of the same person.

"I still haven't been able to question her yet, to clear up a couple of points." Christy started walking toward the exit. "I'm going back up now to check on her one last time before I leave."

"Good, I'll come with you." Annie stayed even with Christy. They had to wait for an elevator and Annie broke the uncomfortable silence. "Did you find more clues?" Annie asked. Christy wasn't making the conversation easy for her.

"Yes. As a matter of fact we did. I had a search warrant when I arrived at her apartment. Don't you think it's odd that it caused her to faint? A guilty conscience maybe?"

"Or lack of food. I know she hadn't been feeling well and didn't eat much, if anything, all day."

"Say what you want to, Annie, but the facts don't lie. You were in her apartment after the body was discovered. Did you notice part of the Easter bunny's costume on the floor?"

Annie shook her head. "How did it get there?"

"Well, that's what I'd like Sylvia to answer. See, I think she wrapped the gun in part of the costume when she shot Forrest, dumped the gun in the toilet tank, but still had the costume piece when you found her in the closet, maybe hidden in her pocket or under her shirt or something. Did you notice all the white fuzzy stuff floating in the tank when you found the gun?"

Annie thought back to that moment. Her eyes opened wide.

"Ah ha! You do remember. Good. I was hoping you could verify that piece of information. Those fibers match the bunny costume. Once Sylvia can communicate, she'd better have a fantastic explanation or, well, you probably don't want to hear what she's in for."

The elevator stopped on the second floor. Christy and Annie were the only ones inside. "You've got it all wrong, Christy. Why wouldn't Sylvia just dump that piece of the costume in the tank with the gun? Get rid of both things at the same time rather than leave it in her apartment? You have to dig deeper on that point."

The elevator door opened. "Okay. Tell me your scenario. I'm ready for a good laugh to hear one of your *theories.*"

Annie ignored Christy's jab. She had to try to get the police to look in a different direction before Sylvia was arrested. "Have you looked into the financial statements for Golden Living? Someone is skimming money from the residents and Sylvia is one of those getting robbed. I can show you her bank statements with big withdrawals just in the past couple of weeks. It doesn't make sense. And from what I learned about how Golden Living gets paid, they get potential new residents to sign over their homes and Golden Living oversees the money. Doesn't that sound suspicious?"

Christy walked out of the elevator. "Why would anyone agree to that?"

"Pressure. Fear. Trusting the wrong person. I don't know, but I heard the pitch and I'm positive they have a scam going on."

"You think Dawn Cross is involved in this?"

"Yes. And I think Forrest was helping her target people, or else he found out and wanted a cut."

"Well, thanks for that tidbit. You just gave Sylvia a strong motive for being in Dawn's office and killing the Easter bunny."

Annie couldn't believe her ears. Christy took her information and twisted it to fit *her* theory like usual. "What I'm telling you is you need to look behind the scene at how the money at Golden Living is being handled. Money that rightly belongs to the residents." Annie was shaking she was so upset. She pointed her finger at Christy. "Before you pin anything on Sylvia, you should do your job thoroughly and follow the money."

Christy's lip twisted up in a snicker. "Wow. Have you slept at all since this murder? You're throwing out some crazy accusations." Christy patted Annie's arm. "I'll ignore that finger you just shoved in my face...this time. But, here's some advice for you, Annie Hunter— go home and get a good night sleep. Let me do *my* job. You never allow yourself to even *consider* the possibility that a friend of yours might actually be capable of the unthinkable."

Annie clenched her jaw. This was so typical of Christy's dismissive attitude but she couldn't stop Annie from digging a little bit more. She got the latest update about Sylvia from the nurse on duty but nothing had changed. With a policeman guarding the door, she realized she wouldn't be getting access to Sylvia anyway.

She hurried back to the elevator and made a beeline to the cafeteria, hoping to find Martha and Marvin still sitting at their table.

For once, something went right. Marvin was carefully cutting a brownie into small pieces with a fork and knife when she pulled out a chair and joined them.

"You look completely exhausted, Martha. If you want to go home, I'll bring Marvin back to Golden Living."

"Are you sure? I know you've had a busy day, too."

Annie patted Martha's hand. "I'm fine. You go home and get some rest."

Martha pushed her chair back. "I'll see you at the café tomorrow morning."

Marvin's head lifted. "Will you pick up more of those hot cross buns for me?"

"Yeah, sure," Martha said, but Annie wasn't sure she'd was paying attention.

"Martha?" Annie said before she was more than a couple steps away. "Do you still have the keys to Sylvia's apartment?"

"I guess I do. Do you want them?" Martha fished around in her purse and pulled out a set of keys. "Here they are. You can give them back to me in the morning."

Annie safely tucked the keys in her pocket. She didn't know what she thought she'd find in Sylvia's apartment, especially after the police probably tore it apart, but it was worth a look now that she knew

Christy was ready to pounce all over Sylvia for murdering Forrest.

"What's your plan with Sylvia's keys?" Marvin eyed Annie suspiciously. "Do you make a habit of trespassing?"

"That's an interesting question, coming from someone who is always snooping around in other people's business," Annie snapped back at Marvin. Who did he think he was, lecturing her when all she was trying to do was help Sylvia?

"I watch and I listen but I don't go into someone's apartment without their permission."

"For your information, Marvin, I do have Sylvia's permission." Sort of. "What do you think I did when I was upstairs?" Annie didn't like lying to Marvin but she didn't want him to mess up her plan. Besides, if Sylvia was innocent, Annie couldn't imagine that she would mind. And if she was guilty, well, then it wouldn't really matter in the long run anyway.

"Oh. In that case, I'll help you." Marvin carefully wiped his lips. "Let's go."

Annie had not anticipated this announcement from Marvin. She only signed on to give Marvin a ride back to Golden Living. Maybe he wouldn't get in the way too much. And, she wouldn't look out of place if she was with someone who lived at Golden Living. She smiled. "Yes, let's go."

Golden Living was well lit up. "Are there a lot of activities going on?" Annie asked Marvin as they approached the main entrance.

"Saturday night Bingo. It's the highlight for plenty of people who live here. That and the organized bus trips to those gambling places."

"Don't you want to play?" Maybe she could get rid of him to the allure of a rousing Bingo game.

"Nope. I never gamble."

So much for that idea. They walked together into Golden Living.

"Is that you, Annie? Where's your four-legged companion?"

Annie squinted to see who was talking to her from one of the doorways. "Gloria? You're working late."

Gloria sighed. "Yes. I had some paperwork to get caught up with. That part of my responsibility got behind with all the uproar and investigations with Forrest's murder. Dawn's around somewhere, too. Plus, we like to make sure the Bingo game doesn't get out of hand."

"Seriously?"

Gloria laughed. "You'd be surprised how competitive some folks are. Even when it's only pennies at stake. Can I help you with something tonight?"

"She's with me," Marvin said and pulled Annie's arm to get her moving again.

Gloria frowned. "Okay then. I hope to see Roxy again soon." She ducked back into her office.

"Does she work late often?" Annie asked Marvin.

"She's here a lot. I don't know if she's always working or just keeping her eyes on things. Come on, the hallway's empty. Where is Sylvia's key? We should get inside without anyone seeing us go in."

Annie jiggled the key in Sylvia's door while Marvin shuffled next to her. "Hurry up before someone comes."

"What difference does it make?" All his nervousness made it harder for Annie to get the door unlocked.

"Just in case."

The door opened and Marvin rushed in before Annie had the key out of the lock. "Holy smokes, this place has been ransacked."

Annie closed the door behind her and surveyed Sylvia's once-tidy apartment. "The police had a search warrant, they must have done this."

"A search warrant? How do you know?"

"I ran into Detective Crank at the hospital. She told me they found part of the Easter bunny costume in here and she's convinced that Sylvia used it to wrap around her gun when she shot Forrest."

Marvin stopped dead in his tracks. "Do you think Sylvia shot Forrest?"

"No. I don't. And I told Detective Crank she needed to look deeper into how Golden Living handles their finances but she thinks it's just another one of my crazy theories."

"We have to take matters into our own hands then, to save Sylvia. We'll have to find the real killer." Marvin stared at Annie as if he expected her to snap her fingers to reveal the evil-doer.

"And what do you think *we* should do next?" Annie wandered around the apartment, picking up cushions, pillows, and clothes that were strewn everywhere. Her toe knocked against some bathroom items. She scooped up toothpaste, shampoo, prescription bottles, and a comb all tangled in a mess of unrolled toilet paper, returning the items back to Sylvia's bathroom.

"I'm wondering about Shady Sean. I know you and Thelma were in his apartment a couple of times. Do you think you can get us back inside?"

"Why?" Annie had an uneasy feeling. Did Marvin also think Sean might be the murderer?

"I saw him going down the hall toward Gloria's office before Forrest was murdered. Maybe he's the killer."

"And what are we going to do if he lets us in his apartment? I don't think that's much of a plan. You have to try to remember who else you saw. You told me that Dawn didn't leave when she told the police she left. I overheard Gloria confirm this, too. Where did you see Dawn?"

"I saw her go out to her car but she didn't drive off. You know, she has a brand new silver BMW. I wonder how she affords *that*. She and Gloria were arguing about something. I couldn't hear, but I could see their arms flying in every direction and fingers pointing. I don't know what either of them did after that because I got distracted when you came charging down the hallway."

Annie put her hands on her hips. "And what about you, Marvin? You didn't like Forrest. You were somewhere near the office. Did you kill him?"

His mouth fell open. His voice trembled quietly. "Forrest wasn't my favorite person but I wouldn't kill him. Or anyone. Not after what I went through. No, I wanted to figure out what he was up to and expose him, let the law take care of him. Let him suffer in jail."

Annie believed him and was glad she finally asked him outright. "We can go try to talk to Sean."

Annie spent several more minutes straightening up more of Sylvia's scattered belongings. With each item she picked up, her anger intensified at the stubbornness and tunnel vision of Detective Crank;

and the urgency she felt to figure out who murdered Forrest Spring.

CHAPTER 24

"Come *on* Annie," Marvin whined, heading for the door to go to Sean's apartment.

"Listen. We do this my way or not at all." Annie needed time to think; preferably without Marvin distracting her. She suddenly had a great idea to get Marvin out of her hair. "You know how Gloria said she's working late tonight?"

Marvin nodded. His face lit up. "I've got an idea. While you finish up here, I'll sneak into the bathroom next to her office and listen in on any conversations."

Exactly Annie's idea, but even better since Marvin figured it out himself. "Perfect, Marvin. Be careful. Don't let anyone see you. Come back if you hear anything interesting."

The door quietly closed behind Marvin giving Annie peace and quiet to think about how to help Sylvia. She didn't come up with much before there was a knock on Sylvia's door.

"Geesh, Marvin, couldn't you hang out in the bathroom for a bit longer?" But it wasn't Marvin looking at Annie when she pulled the door open.

"Annie? I saw the lights and thought Sylvia was back."

The hairs on Annie's neck rose. "Dawn. Maybe I can help you with something?"

Dawn walked into Sylvia's apartment and closed the door. "Maybe. How is she doing? I haven't been able to get away to visit her."

"The police are guarding her room. That's all I know."

Dawn's eyes opened wide. "Why?" Her eyes darted around but most of the mess was picked up.

"You'll have to ask Detective Crank yourself. I came to pick up some things to bring back to the hospital for her."

"Oh." Dawn rubbed her arm. "I wanted to talk to her about this apartment."

Annie waited, hoping Dawn would elaborate.

"I guess I'll have to wait until she returns."

"Have her return to her home so you can throw her out?" Annie's words fell out before she could think. "How do you sleep at night, Dawn Cross? How can you treat these elderly people so cruelly?"

"What are you talking about?" She took a step closer to Annie.

"Stealing Sylvia's money. That's what I'm talking about. I saw her bank statements with big chunks of money withdrawn. For what? Did you think no one would figure out your scam?"

Dawn's eyes narrowed. She reached her hand toward Annie but Annie backed away, keeping Sylvia's small table between herself and Dawn. Annie's heart pounded.

Sylvia's door opened and Annie had never been so happy to see Marvin. "Are you all right, Annie?"

"Yes...Dawn was just leaving."

"You two...never mind." Dawn slinked from the apartment and Annie sank onto Sylvia's rocking chair.

"What was that all about?" Marvin checked that the door was locked and sat down across from Annie.

"I honestly don't know. She said she thought Sylvia was here and wanted to talk to her."

"Harumph. That's one big fat lie. I heard Dawn complaining to Gloria about how you're messing up the deal with Thelma Dodd. Once they stopped talking, I came back here to warn you."

This confirmed what Annie thought about how Dawn pressured people to sign their house away. These people had no morals and they had to be stopped.

"I'm ready to go visit Sean. But please, try to keep your comments to yourself. I don't think Sean is a bad guy."

Marvin scowled but kept quiet all the way to Sean's apartment door.

Annie knocked.

They waited.

And waited.

"What do we do now?" Marvin asked.

Annie shrugged. She really had no idea what to do next. What she would *like* to do was head home to escape this crazy place but running away wasn't an option if she wanted to stop Dawn.

Marvin knocked. "Open up, Sean. Annie has some important information."

"Will he listen to you? I thought you two didn't get along."

Marvin shrugged. "We have a good act going, don't we?" His lips twitched up at the edges.

The door opened.

"It's late." Sean's wheelchair blocked the door.

"Let us in before Dawn or Gloria sees us here." Marvin took a step inside. "They're already keeping a close eye on Annie. We don't have much time to fix this mess."

Sean moved back into his apartment. "Do we have to do this now? I was about to go to bed."

Annie looked between Sean and Marvin. "What the heck is going on? You two are friends? What else isn't what it seems around here?"

"Sit down, Annie. There's a lot you don't know," Sean said. "I'll put the kettle on. Tea?"

Annie sat. Her head was spinning. What was she doing in this apartment with these two men? Either one could be a killer. No one knew she was here. Were they working together to find Forrest's killer or working together to keep her from continuing her search?

"We had to be sure you weren't connected to the management here." Sean looked at Marvin. "One of us is slightly paranoid, but when you showed up with Thelma, I knew you could be trusted. Thelma is the best judge of character of all the people I've known over the years. Marvin wasn't convinced though. I was surprised to see you at my door tonight. What happened to change your mind, Marvin?"

"The look on Annie's face when I walked into Sylvia's apartment just now. Pure terror that Dawn was planning to harm her. Annie was actually happy to see me for a change, right?"

Annie let herself relax slightly. "Yes, Marvin. I wanted to kiss you on both cheeks. But I still don't know what's going on."

"Both cheeks, huh? Not sure I want all that slobber on my face." Marvin brought the tea to the table. "The rest of those brownies would go good with this. I'll get them from Sylvia's apartment."

"You didn't eat them all already?" Annie teased.

The door quietly clicked as Marvin left without answering Annie's question.

Sean had some papers spread on the table. "I'll see if I can explain things to you. I found something interesting with Sylvia's bank statements. Those withdrawals didn't go to Golden Living."

Annie waited, her hand suspended in midair. Her stomach clenched in a knot. "Where did they go?" She held her breath, waiting for his answer.

"To Forrest Spring."

"Why?" This was not at all what she'd expected to hear.

"I don't know the answer to that question, but I'm sure I'm right about this. I have Forrest's account information from when I bought something from him and did a money transfer from my account to his."

"If those money transfers mean Forrest was blackmailing Sylvia about something, it only reinforces her motive to kill him." Annie sipped her tea. "Do you think she *is* the murderer?"

"Annie, I wish I knew. My gut tells me no, but she does have that history of killing her husband in her past. Maybe she felt she had no other option." Sean rubbed the stubble on his chin. "And we can't exactly ask Forrest, can we."

"Sylvia seemed to like Forrest and he was not a fan of the management here. Maybe she was trying to help him financially? Is that even a remote possibility?"

"I thought of that, too, but she really wasn't in the position to help him financially. We can only wait until she can answer that question herself. For now, we have to figure out how to keep her out of jail," Sean said.

"What have you put together so far?" Annie asked.

"Not much unfortunately. All I know is that people here are losing money hand over fist. I'm trying to stay in the background until I'm positive what's going on so the mastermind doesn't get tipped off. What do *you* know?"

"Just a bunch of theories without any evidence to back them up."

"Let's start with that."

Annie took a deep breath. At least she didn't think Sean would ridicule her like Christy always did. "Sylvia told me she saw a pile of cash in Dawn's safe sometime on Wednesday but it was gone when I found Forrest's body. Dawn told me that she deposited the money into the Catfish Credit Union. I told this to Detective Crank but I don't know if she will follow up on it."

He opened a notebook and jotted down some notes. "Something to follow, where did the money go? What else?"

"While I was finishing cleaning up after the Easter dinner, Forrest told me he was going to Dawn's office to get paid. Here's where I've tried to make something plausible out of what happened. Sylvia was in Dawn's office and heard someone coming, probably Forrest, so she hid in the closet."

"Why did she go to the office in the first place?"

"She said she needed to talk to Dawn about her financial problems."

Sean drew a line on his paper and made more notes. "Go on."

"Sylvia heard a gunshot. She texted Martha. We— Martha, my mother, and myself—were still finishing up in the kitchen and we ran to Dawn's office. The door was closed and the lights were off. I carefully cracked open the door and reached in, feeling for the light. Once I peeked around the corner, I heard a sob and found Sylvia in the closet."

"What about Forrest?"

"He was dead on the floor behind Dawn's desk. I didn't see him at first because I was helping Sylvia. Martha saw him. We called the police."

"That's pretty straight forward, but not good for Sylvia."

"Right."

Sean looked toward his door. "What's taking Marvin so long? Did he say he was going to *bake* some brownies?"

Annie laughed. "No. I gave him a bag of brownies that he said he left in Sylvia's apartment. Should I go look for him?"

"Probably or he'll eat them all himself. I've never known anyone with a bigger sweet tooth. I'll work on the timeline while you're gone, adding in what you've told me to what I know."

Sean tore out a clean sheet of paper and was lost in his work by the time Annie pushed herself away from the table. She walked to Sylvia's apartment, glad to see that the hallway was deserted. She pushed the door open. It was dark. She stood perfectly still and listened.

Silence.

"Marvin?" she whispered. "Are you in here?"

Silence.

Where did he go?

Annie flipped the light switch up. Sylvia's apartment filled with brightness. She walked in and scanned the area. No Marvin. She checked the bedroom and bathroom. No Marvin. He must have gone to his apartment for some reason. To eat the brownies in secret? Annie hoped it was something that simple.

CHAPTER 25

Annie left Sylvia's apartment and turned to lock the door.

"Annie, I didn't know you were still here." Annie almost jump out of her skin. "I thought you already left with Sylvia's things. Did you find everything you need?"

"Oh...Dawn." Annie's hand flew to her chest. "You startled me. "Yes, I...uh, already put her things in my car but I wasn't sure whether I remembered to lock the door."

"Great. I'll walk you back to your car since I'm finally on my way home, too." Dawn smiled and waited for Annie.

"Oh...um...I have to tell Marvin what time I'll be back to take him to the hospital to see Sylvia tomorrow." She stood in the hallway, hoping Dawn would accept her flimsy excuse for not leaving yet on top of her lie about putting Sylvia's things in her car.

"Just send him a text message." Dawn kept her eyes on Annie's face.

Annie laughed nervously. "He gets confused with his phone. I'd better just pop over and tell him in person." She started walking toward Marvin's apartment, desperate to get out from under Dawn's glare. She forced herself to act cool, calm, and collected when she really wanted to make a mad dash for safety.

"Okay. Good night, then." Dawn's voice echoed in the deserted hall.

Annie could hear the tap of Dawn's shoes receding. She glanced over her shoulder to be sure Dawn was moving away from her before she knocked on Marvin's door. No answer. Where was he?

At the end of the hall, Sean's door creaked open and Marvin's face popped through the crack. "Psst...Annie." Marvin waved her toward the open door. She gratefully slipped inside, willing her heartbeat to calm.

"What did Dawn want?" Marvin asked.

Annie moved toward a chair, hoping her trembling legs would support her long enough to get to it. "I don't know, but she appeared behind me and scared me out of my skin again."

"That's the second time tonight she crept up on you. Maybe you should head home and get away from this place."

"Dawn said she was going home so I shouldn't run into her again tonight." Annie looked at Sean. "How's that timeline coming along?"

He slid the paper across the table. "There are a lot of holes, but Marvin did add some more pieces."

Annie focused on the paper, reading it slowly, top to bottom, before she looked up. "So, you both think Dawn killed Forrest?"

"We put her at the top of the list," Sean explained. "One, the safe was open in her office. Two, she knew Forrest would be stopping by to get paid. Three, she lied to the police about the time she left, according to what Marvin saw. And four, she's the one who controls all the paperwork about the people who live here so she'd have that biggest motive to silence anyone who was onto her scheme."

Annie didn't disagree with anything Sean said, especially after overhearing Dawn and Gloria's conversation about letting Sylvia take the fall. *But*, she saw a few holes. "How did Dawn get Sylvia's gun?"

"It's possible that she broke into Sylvia's apartment and stole it. Sylvia never reported it being missing and there have been quite a few break-ins recently. As a matter of fact, someone broke into my apartment when I was gone to a doctor's appointment."

"What is getting stolen?"

"No one is sure, but they can tell a drawer was rifled through or a couch cushion was knocked to the floor. In my case, a whole folder of papers was missing."

That answer surprised Annie. She thought she might have to confess to taking one paper from Sean's desk.

Apparently someone else was interested in what Sean was doing and stole the whole folder.

"Were they important papers?"

Sean laughed. "I guess someone thought so. They were actually copies of papers from Dawn's safe but I hadn't uncovered any useful information."

"Maybe I shouldn't ask, but how did you get papers from Dawn's safe?"

"You're right, you shouldn't ask." Sean had a smile on his face, but Annie knew she would not get any more information from him.

Annie took that to mean she should stop asking questions so she brought the conversation back to Sylvia. "Let's say Dawn shot Forrest while Sylvia was hiding in the closet. Then what did she do?"

"She left through the door connecting Dawn and Gloria's offices and hid the gun in the toilet tank before she left through the outside door in Gloria's office." Sean raised both palms. "It's the best I've got."

"That seems unlikely that she'd be able to get in and out of the bathroom without being seen." Annie pointed at Marvin. "You were around watching stuff and you didn't see her go to the bathroom, did you?"

"No," Marvin answered hesitantly. "But maybe she didn't hide the gun in the toilet tank until the next day. She could have left with it, wrapped in part of the

Easter bunny costume, and brought it back, waiting for the right moment to dump the gun in the tank and plant the costume in Sylvia's apartment."

"But why bring it back? That seems way too risky." Annie shook her head.

Sean rubbed his chin thoughtfully. "Dawn obviously wanted to frame Sylvia. It would make her look much guiltier if the gun was found somewhere in Golden Living. Sylvia wouldn't be able to get rid of it elsewhere very easily."

Annie sat back in her chair and sighed heavily. "An awful lot of ifs would have to fall into place for your timeline to work perfectly. And with Dawn going in and out through Gloria's office, where was Gloria during all this?"

Both Marvin and Sean shrugged.

"I saw her outside with Dawn before all the chaos, but then I lost track of her," Marvin admitted.

"Did you actually see Dawn come back inside?"

Marvin shook his head and helped himself to the last brownie.

Annie pushed Sean's timeline back across the table to him. "If you look at all this from the point of view of the police, I hate to say it, but Sylvia certainly looks like the killer. We're trying to make something fit because that's what we *want* to happen." She stood.

"There has to be some other piece of evidence or I just don't think Sylvia has a chance to beat this."

"We can't give up on her," Marvin said. "My common sense just knows she didn't do it." His eyes pleaded with Annie.

"I agree, but it doesn't matter if we can't find the missing piece to prove it was someone else. As a matter of fact, when I first started looking into all this, I thought either you, Marvin, or you, Sean, could have been the killer. You both were near Dawn's and Gloria's offices."

"What are you talking about?" Sean said. "I didn't even get close to the offices when I went to pick up my dinner. The police were already swarming the halls. I told them that I was trying to get my dinner and they told me too bad. It was part of a crime scene and to get back to my own apartment."

"You never got the stuffed zucchini I made special for that night?" Annie wondered if Gloria ended up eating hers and Sean's, or maybe one of the policemen ate it.

"Stuffed zucchini? Now I'm hungry. I wouldn't say no to a raincheck." Sean actually smiled at Annie, a smile that caused the corners of his eyes to crinkle, and she realized he had a kind face when it wasn't pulled into his usual scowl.

Annie yawned and stretched her arms over her head. "I'm going home. I don't know what else we can do but tomorrow's another day and, maybe after a good night's sleep, some new angle will show itself."

"You haven't given up, have you?" Marvin asked, his voice filled with worry.

"Not at all, but I can't think about this anymore tonight. If I give my brain a rest, I'm hoping I can see this puzzle in a new light tomorrow. Either Martha or I will pick you up if you want to visit Sylvia."

"I'll be here, ready and waiting. And I think Martha promised to bring hot cross buns," Marvin added.

"You asked for some but I don't recall hearing a promise. You'll have to wait and see," Annie teased. She was surprised how quickly Marvin's quirky personality had grown on her. He really was like a pesky guard dog. Not a big tough German shepherd, but a small, yippy, ankle-biting rat terrier, who always showed up in the nick of time. She couldn't stand his crestfallen face. "I'll be sure you get your hot cross buns tomorrow."

Marvin's smile was a satisfying way to end her day, she thought, as she closed Sean's apartment door and walked down the long hall toward the main entrance.

Light glowed from Gloria's open office door. Was she still working? Annie peeked into the office to give Gloria the stuffed zucchini recipe she had promised to share. Gloria wasn't around. Probably better that way for a quicker exit and return home.

As Annie scribbled a note to attach to the recipe, the door from Dawn's office opened. "Oh, Annie, I'm glad you're still here. Dawn read me the riot act that I never got you to fill in the proper papers for your visits with Roxy." Gloria let out a little laugh. "You know, for insurance."

"Okay." Annie decided to use this opportunity to dig some information out of Gloria. "About Dawn, you said you were keeping your eyes on her. She was pretty ruthless with her pressure to get Thelma to sign her intent to move in. Is that normal?"

Gloria sat at her desk and leaned on her elbows toward Annie. "Unfortunately, it is. I shouldn't be blabbing but I like you. The president of Golden Living wants this place full at all times. You know, maximum profits for him, so he gives a signing bonus."

"Does that pit you and Dawn against each other?" Annie was flabbergasted at Gloria's information.

"Sort of, and I was ticked off when I thought I would get the opportunity to sign Thelma but Dawn said I could have the next candidate. It's much better if we work together. Plus, she *is* my boss."

"I see." Annie didn't really see much of anything except more questions. "And most people use their home equity for payment?"

"That's not uncommon."

"You know," Annie used Gloria's words to pretend some sort of camaraderie, "I'm only asking these questions to help Thelma with her decision."

"Of course. Ask away." Gloria sat back, crossed her legs, and waited as if she had all night to entertain Annie.

"Okay. Here's the thing. I've heard some chatter that many residents are going through their money much faster than expected. To be blunt, is everything above board here?"

Gloria leaned forward again. She had a gleam in her eyes. "I've wondered the same thing but I'm not privy to the financials for the residents."

"Do you think someone is skimming money out of these people's accounts?"

Gloria raised her eyebrows and shrugged. "It's a valid question but without access to where the money is going, I don't have an answer. If I was your friend, Thelma, I'd be sure to have a good lawyer check all the paperwork before she signs anything." She laughed. "But you didn't hear that from me."

Annie stood. "I can't help but wonder if any of this is connected to why Forrest was murdered. Do you have any theories?"

"Forrest was a busybody and my guess is that he pissed off the wrong person." Gloria's voice had a slight undertone of disgust.

"Right. And that's what bothers me with all this attention on Sylvia. What could he have done to upset her enough to kill him?"

Gloria stood also. "Poor Sylvia. All I know is that the police think they have an airtight case against her. Such a shame."

"I almost forgot." Annie pointed to the recipe card on Gloria's desk. "The whole reason I popped in here was to leave you the stuffed zucchini recipe."

"Wonderful. I just loved it." Gloria walked around her desk with the papers for Annie to sign.

Annie skimmed the form in front of her saying Golden Living would not be responsible if the visiting animal caused harm to anyone. By signing, Annie agreed to accept all responsibility. She wasn't convinced this would hold up in court if anything happened and someone wanted to sue Golden Living but that wouldn't be her problem. She signed the form.

"By the way," Gloria said, "Sean loved the stuffed zucchini, too. He couldn't say enough about what a treat it was from the normal cafeteria vegetarian offerings, when the cook even remembers to make him something."

"When did Sean get the meal? I thought he told me he never got it." Annie shook her tired head. There was too much to keep straight.

Gloria tittered a high pitched quick laugh. "Oh, we must have discussed a different night. Maybe it was the eggplant parmesan he said he loved so much."

As Annie turned to hand the form to Gloria, she accidentally bumped into a canvas tote bag sitting right on the edge of the desk. The contents spilled all over the floor. "Sorry." She immediately bent down to retrieve the items.

"Oh, my container that I gave you the stuffed zucchini in. I use this all the time. I'd forgotten that you had it and I wondered what I did with it." As Annie picked it up, something inside rattled around.

Gloria held her hand out. "Sorry I didn't return that yet. I have a few items stored inside. It'll only take me a minute to find something else to put it in."

"Here, I'll just dump it all into your tote." Annie, not wanting to wait for Gloria to find something else, pulled the yellow silicone cover off. Comprehension was slow for her tired brain. What was she looking at? "This is an awful lot of medicine."

Gloria tried to take the container but only managed to spill all the pill bottles on the floor.

Annie reached down to help pick them up. Her fingers tightened around a bottle and the name *Sean*

Woodman almost jumped off the label to her eyes. "Huh?" Her heart pounded. Her body tingled with a surge of adrenaline. Her fingers shook.

Annie felt like she was standing in the twilight zone.

She looked at Gloria who, instead of cleaning up what spilled on the floor, held a heavy ceramic potted plant above Annie's head.

Gloria's face was drained of color. "I wish you hadn't done that, Annie. Everything was falling into place so well, and I did enjoy your visits with your dog."

As the pot crashed toward Annie's skull, a body charged into the room and knocked Gloria down. The potted spider plant sailed inches past Annie's head and shattered on the floor. Another shape moved at the edge of Annie's vision. By the time her brain caught up with the events happening around her, she saw Marvin on the floor struggling with Gloria. Sean, close behind, maneuvered his wheelchair so it straddled as much of Gloria's prone body as possible, allowing Marvin to roll free.

Annie stared at the two unlikely heroes. "I should have suspected something was up when Gloria told me how much you loved the stuffed zucchini, Sean. But she covered it up pretty well with talk of an eggplant parmesan meal instead."

"When Marvin saw you walk into Gloria's office, we decided we should listen to your conversation." He shook his head. "We haven't had eggplant parmesan for weeks and I told Marvin. He put two and two together just in time."

Annie fumbled to get her phone from her pocket but her trembling fingers didn't want to obey her brain.

"Hurry up, Annie. I don't know how long I can keep Gloria under control," Sean said. He tried to hold the wheels steady over Gloria's thrashing legs.

"Don't worry." Marvin jumped on her back and pressed his hands on her shoulders. "She won't get away if it's the last thing I do."

Annie finally managed to punch in Detective Crank's number, forgetting that calling 911 might be the better option. "You need to get over to Golden Living as soon as possible," she blurted out without any greeting.

"Annie? What's going on? Is there another death?" Christy asked. Her voice held concern without a trace of sarcasm for a change.

"Not yet, but there might be if you don't hurry." Annie hung up. That was sure to get Christy speeding across town.

CHAPTER 26

Annie had all the pill bottles lined up on the edge of Gloria's desk. It just seemed like the right thing to do. And it kept her busy while she, Marvin, and Sean counted the seconds for the police to arrive.

Sean read the labels—none were prescribed to Gloria Knight. Instead, every single bottle had the name of an elderly resident living at Golden Living clearly printed on the label.

"You were responsible for all the break-ins, Gloria?" Annie wanted to give her a good kick in the side but with Marvin still sitting on her, she decided that was enough humiliation.

With her face smashed into the carpet, all she managed was a grunt.

"I think I've discovered the answer to who Forrest pissed off. He discovered your little robbery sideline, didn't he?" Annie demanded. When Gloria didn't respond, she nudged her arm with her foot. "*Didn't* he?" she asked louder.

Gloria shifted her head enough to give her mouth some space. "Of course he had to be a do-gooder and cozy up to a bunch of the people that live here. I never took *all* the pain meds, just a few here and there," Gloria whined.

Annie's anger simmered close to the boiling point. "And that made it okay?" She didn't expect a reply to that question. "Finding Sylvia's gun on one of your little break-ins made for a perfect set up. All you needed was the opportunity to find Forrest all alone, and Dawn gave you that. You knew she planned to skip out without writing his check Wednesday night. It was just a matter of timing."

Detective Crank finally marched into Gloria's office. "I hope you have a good explanation for hanging up on me, Annie. What's going on in here?"

Annie pointed to the pill bottles lined up on Gloria's desk next to her container and the yellow silicone lid. "This ought to be a good starting point. Apparently, Gloria's addiction got the better of her, but she slipped up tonight."

"Oh?"

"It's hard to keep the lies straight. She forgot that Sean never got his special vegetarian meal from the Easter dinner on Wednesday night. She also forgot she used *my* reusable container to store her stolen drugs." Annie shook her head. "That, along with the minor detail that she tried to smash my head to pieces to shut me up, should be enough to lock her up."

"And you two?" Christy turned her attention to Marvin and Sean.

"Eye witnesses. And I knocked Gloria over," Marvin said, his chest puffed full of pride.

"Yes. Marvin is the hero here tonight," Annie said. "He saved my life." She looked at Marvin who had tears in his eyes. "Thank you, Marvin." Annie felt her eyes fill, too. She hoped that finally he might be able to let go of what happened all those years ago in his past and realize that all you can do is your best.

Detective Crank took charge, letting Annie, Marvin, and Sean leave the office with the promise of getting a complete statement on Monday.

"That's one mystery solved, but it doesn't explain the disappearing money," Sean said as the three stood in the hallway.

"I think it will be easier to track all that down now," Annie said. "At least, I *hope* Detective Crank finally takes that issue seriously." She hugged Marvin and patted Sean's shoulder. "You both are amazing. I'm exhausted, but I'll see you tomorrow." She started to walk toward the door with her mind focused on falling into bed.

"You're not so bad yourself, Annie," Marvin said. "Don't forget you promised to bring me some more of those hot cross buns."

When she turned around, his grin reached from ear to ear.

The lights streaming from the windows of her house when she pulled into the driveway felt like a kiss from an old friend. But she knew she would have to face Jason and explain what happened.

His face was a mask when she walked inside.

"You already heard?"

"Marvin called Martha and Martha called Leona and Leona called Mia and Mia called me. At least, I think that was how it went." He wrapped his arms around Annie. "I was terrified when Mia called."

"Yeah, well, Gloria was stealing pain meds from the people living at Golden Living and Forrest found out about her activity. I don't know if he was blackmailing her or threatening to go to the police, but whatever happened, she decided she needed to silence him."

"With Sylvia's gun?"

"Yup. I guess she stole that, too."

"And the missing money?"

Annie shrugged. "That one's still a mystery but I suspect Christy will dig around and get to the bottom of it now."

"Are you tired?"

"Exhausted."

He led her to the stairs. "You'd better get some sleep. Leona has an Easter brunch planned and you aren't allowed to miss it."

Annie groaned as she dragged herself up the stairs. Her legs were harder to lift with each step. She wasn't at all sure she would wake up in time for Leona's brunch.

It turned out that waking up wasn't an issue because Jason pulled the warm comforter off at ten the next morning. "I let you sleep in long enough. Time to rise and shine, Mrs. Hunter."

Annie groaned, rolled over, and put her pillow over her head.

That got yanked off, too. "Hop in the shower. I've got coffee ready before we head over to the Black Cat Café."

Annie groaned for the third time but she slipped her feet to the floor and managed to get herself into the shower. The hot water helped to wash the last of the exhaustion away. With comfy jeans and a bright yellow t-shirt with an Easter bunny eating a dandelion, as a memento to Forrest, she joined Jason in their kitchen.

"Here you go. One cup of extra strong, dark roast coffee. I added a swirl of cream."

Annie sat at one of the kitchen stools with her hands wrapped around the warm mug. "What's happening at the café? Can't we say we forgot and blow it off?"

"I don't think that would be a good idea. You know how Leona is. She'd probably come get you if we don't show up."

"Okay, okay." She rinsed her mug and looked out the window. "At least it's a beautiful day. Look at that bright blue sky."

The parking lot at the café was pretty full. But it was Easter Sunday, after all. Everyone was probably picking up cakes and hot cross buns for family get-togethers.

Jason and Annie walked arm-in-arm into the café.

Annie stopped suddenly, her arm coming loose from Jason's elbow when he kept walking.

One booth was filled with four people she didn't expect to see at the café. Thelma, Sylvia, Marvin, and Sean were all chatting happily. Leona and Mia fussed over Annie, hugging her, and checking that she was truly still in one piece.

"What's going on?"

"Brunch. Get yourself a plate and help yourself to the food," Leona said.

The counter was overflowing with two types of egg casseroles, quiches, sausages, freshly squeezed orange juice, sliced fruit, and Leona's special hot cross buns.

Annie whispered to Jason, "Whose idea was this?"

"Marvin. After you left Golden Living last night, Christy told him that Sylvia was feeling better and obviously, with Gloria arrested, Sylvia was free to go back to her apartment once the hospital released her. He decided a celebration was in order."

Annie suddenly felt ravenous and she piled a plate with some of every item before she and Jason sat together at the booth next to her friends. Just as she had a forkful of quiche ready to tickle her taste buds, Detective Crank slid in next to her.

"You sure know how to ruin my appetite," Annie said.

"Nice to see you, too. Don't go anywhere. I'm getting some coffee, then I'll be back to talk to you."

Annie looked at Jason. Jason shrugged. "This wasn't part of the plan as far as I know."

Christy returned with her coffee and a hot cross bun. "I couldn't resist something to go with my coffee." She took a big bite, then tested her coffee. "Ah, still too hot." She sat back in the booth. "So, I thought you might like to hear what happened after you left last night."

Annie waited.

"Just as I was driving out, I saw a silver BMW pull into the parking lot. I had always wondered how Dawn managed to afford such an expensive car, so I waited for her to park and go inside before I returned. You'll never guess what she was doing." Christy sipped her coffee. "Returning a pile of cash to the safe."

"Returning it?"

"Yeah, she said she had taken it by mistake or some lame excuse like that. I told her I'd consider letting it slide if she explained who was skimming money from some of the accounts."

"What if it was her?"

"Then she was in big trouble. She peeped like a little chick and handed over all the financial papers. It was her boss that pressured her to find residents and get them to sign over their houses for a nice bonus for her, but he was the one to control the accounts and skim off the money. So, I think everything's all cleaned up over at Golden Living. Well, it will be once they find some new management."

"There's still one mystery," Annie said. She leaned over to the booth and looked at Sylvia. "Why did you give Forrest so much money?" She couldn't quite make sense of the big withdrawals from Sylvia's account.

She looked at each of her friends. "He told me he was trying to protect it for me once he found out about how Golden Living was taking our money. I was too embarrassed to tell any of you about what I did, and now I don't think I can ever get it back. I don't know where I'll live."

Christy stood and moved closer to Sylvia. "Do you have any paperwork from Forrest?"

Sylvia nodded. "Oh yes. He gave me a receipt for every penny I signed over to him."

"Get all that paperwork to me and I'll see what I can do to fix that mess. What with everything else that was going on at Golden Living, I don't want you to worry anymore."

Sean handed Sylvia a wrapped package.

"What's this?" She turned it over and over in her hand.

"Open it," Sean said.

Sylvia pulled the tape off the ends and slid her Norma Rockwell lithograph from the brown wrapping. Her eyes sparkled. "How much do I owe you?" she managed to whisper.

"Nothing. I was always just keeping it safe for the right moment to return it to you." Sean helped himself to another forkful of quiche.

Christy patted Sylvia's shoulder and walked to the counter, grabbing another hot cross bun on her way out.

"I can't believe everything is sorted out, then." Annie said. She felt a warm glow fill her chest.

"Not everything," Mia said.

The café door opened and Martha walked in with a small brown dog of nondescript breed. He pranced with plenty of energy and his ears perked up as soon as he entered. With a yip, he pulled away from Martha and ran straight to Marvin.

"Scout!" Marvin practically fell off the seat in his haste to greet his dog. Scout jumped into Marvin's arms and licked his face.

Annie grinned from ear to ear. "Now, everything is sorted out."

A Note from Lyndsey

Thank you for reading my cozy mystery, *Easter Buried Eggs.*

Never miss a release date and sign up for my newsletter here—http://LyndseyColeBooks.com

ABOUT THE AUTHOR

Lyndsey Cole lives in New England in a small rural town with her husband who puts up with all the characters in her head, her dog who hogs the couch, her cat who is the boss, and 3 chickens that would like to move into the house. She surrounds herself with gardens full of beautiful perennials. Sitting among the flowers with the scent of lilac, peonies, lily of the valley, or whatever is in bloom, stimulates her imagination about who will die next!

OTHER BOOKS BY LYNDSEY COLE

The Hooked & Cooked Series

Gunpowder Chowder

Mobsters and Lobsters

A Fishy Dish

Crook, Line and Sinker

Catch of the Dead

The Black Cat Café Series

BlueBuried Muffins

StrawBuried in Chocolate

BlackBuried Pie

Very Buried Cheesecake

RaspBuried Torte

PoisonBuried Punch

CranBuried Coffee Cake

WineBuried Wedding

Jingle Buried Cookies

The Lily Bloom Series

Begonias Mean Beware

Queen of Poison

Roses are Dead

Drowning in Dahlias

Hidden by the Hydrangeas

Christmas Tree Catastrophe